LOVE IN MODENA

A DESERT LOVE NOVELLA

ANGELINA KALAHARI

PRAISE FOR LOVE IN MODENA

"Often I am left with a feeling of 'what happened after' in romance books, and it was really refreshing to read a follow-up story." – Mary Anne Yarde, author of the Du Lac Chronicles.

To soulmates everywhere

FlameProjects

Publisher's Note: This is a work of fiction. Names, characters, places, and incidents are a product of the author's imagination. Locales and public names are sometimes used for atmospheric purposes. Any resemblance to actual people, living or dead, or to businesses, companies, events, institutions, or locales is completely coincidental.

Love In Modena – 1st ed.
ISBN 978-0-9954877-3-4

THANK YOU

For buying
Love in Modena

I hope you enjoy reading the novel as much as I've enjoyed
writing it.
To receive occasional email notifications about freebies, new
stories and novels, YouTube videos, short stories and much more,
please go to the end of this book for details on how to get in
touch.

CHAPTER 1

*T*heir home. Hers and Luca's.

Naomi sighed her contentment.

The villa felt like a cozy nest despite its size. Love makes a house a home, Auntie Elsa had always said, and Naomi couldn't agree more.

The love she shared with Luca was like nothing she could've imagined. It was so much better on every level. None of the romances she'd liked to read as a teenager had prepared her for the joy that overflowed in smiles that refused to leave her face, even at the most inappropriate moments. She knew the light that enveloped her soul now was one she'd never want to lose.

She stretched out her legs in front of her and reclined on the sunbed.

How amazing to think the same sun shining here on her in Italy was the one that had shone on her in her beloved Namibia. It felt different here, somehow, though. Softer, friendlier with none of the harshness of the desert, but none of its underlying excitement, either.

Naomi took a sip from the iced drink that stood on the small table next to her sunbed.

At least, this part of life reminded her of life in Namibia when, on days off, most people liked to relax next to a swimming pool with a drink in hand. She'd have to hold Luca to the swimming pool he'd promised to build her.

When Naomi had first laid eyes on the sun trap the balcony outside her new bedroom had created, she'd ordered two sun loungers and an umbrella for the balcony. She'd envisaged the two of them spending time here together, relaxing and prolonging the vacation mood of their honeymoon for as long as possible.

Once she got used to being in Italy and work took over, the initial feeling of being on vacation would evaporate. Such a shame Luca rarely joined her here, though. Instead, he seemed hell-bent on having her vacation mood last by showing off as much of the surrounding area as he could.

On his days off, they'd drive around in one of his Armati sports cars. He'd hold her hand on his thigh and chat enthusiastically as the breath-taking Italian landscapes whizzed past. Invariably, they'd end up at some little family-run restaurant where everyone knew him. Good-naturedly, they'd accept her into their bosom with gusto and serve the best food Naomi had ever eaten.

She'd have to watch her waistline with all these delicious meals. It was one reason she looked forward to her daily meeting with Santina when the two women could enjoy the almost private pool facilities at Armati HQ.

Naomi realized she must've fallen asleep when her alarm alerted her to the imminent arrival of her Italian language coach. She grabbed her floral caftan and walked through the sumptuous bedroom.

How could her eyes not be drawn to the bed, their bed? Luca had ordered a brand-new super king size bed for them to share now they were married. Like her old one at Desert Lodge, this was a safe place. At Desert Lodge, her bed was her sanctuary from the ever-present guests. Here it was her escape from a culture she didn't understand yet, and a safe place to reconnect with who she was in this exotic world she'd hoped to inhabit properly one day.

Now, it had become a place of wanton abandon in the arms of her lover and husband. It was where their trust in one another expressed itself in the way they loved each other, where Luca taught her what he liked and where they experimented to find out what she liked.

Yes, it was again her oasis in life, but oh, what an oasis.

She hurried down the corridor towards the double marble staircase that ran through the center of the impressive foyer.

At first, the house had taken some getting used to. It differed greatly from Desert Lodge. The grand old German house at the edge of the Namib Desert was all she'd known as home. It was where she'd spent most of her young life after Auntie Elsa and Uncle Wouter had adopted her following the tragic death of her parents.

Luca had told her his house in Italy - theirs after their wedding in the desert - was big and full of marble. He hadn't exaggerated. It was much bigger than she'd imagined. Her impression upon first sight was that the interior consisted entirely of marble. The massive double marble staircase connecting the upper rooms with the foyer was only the beginning. Countertops and tiles in the bathrooms and kitchen also sported the finest marble, as did the floor in the foyer.

Luca had been worried it was too much, or it would feel too cold, but Naomi had loved it immediately. Once she'd seen it, she couldn't imagine Luca living anywhere else. As he was now hers, she wanted to be where he was, and with touches from her here and there, she'd transformed the villa into a home for them. Despite its size, it felt cozy and welcoming. Luca had teased she might have to consider a career as an interior designer as she'd done such a good job in their home.

As Naomi came down the staircase, she could see Francisca's silhouette through the frosted glass of the front door.

Luca had beamed when she'd told him she'd wanted to learn his language. He'd wasted no time finding the best language coach in the area. In a surprisingly short time, Francisca had helped Naomi to get to grips with Italian.

At first, Naomi couldn't even make out where one word stopped, and a new one began. But now, four months later, it was making sense. Occasionally, when feeling brave, she'd ordered items and meals in Italian and was amazed when people actually understood her.

An hour later, just as her lesson with Francisca ended, Naomi heard Santina's melodic voice as her mother-in-law opened the front door.

Santina had always had a key to Luca's home, and there was no reason to change that arrangement now Naomi and Luca were married.

"Naomi! Are you home?"

Santina knew Naomi was home, but it was her habit every day to call out the same phrase upon entering. It had quickly become a token of comfort to Naomi in her new life.

Naomi hugged Francisca thank you, and together they walked from the library to meet Santina in the foyer. Santina was admiring the enormous bouquet of lilies in a Murano glass vase on top of the round marble table in the foyer.

She looked up when Naomi and Francisca came into the foyer.

"Ah, there you are. Hello, Francisca. These are gorgeous, Naomi. And they smell so lovely."

Naomi smiled and went to hug Santina.

"Aren't they just? A gift from Luca."

With arms around each other, they waved Francisca off through the open front door.

Naomi felt blessed that Santina was in their lives in this

way. But Santina's arm around Naomi's waist somehow transported her back to that moment Luca had discovered Santina was his birth mother instead of Cecilia. Naomi knew it could've gone terribly wrong. Luca had been furious, feeling he'd been lied to all his life. Naomi knew he'd been blaming himself for years for Cecilia's disappearance, convinced she'd left because of him. His young mind couldn't imagine anything else for her departure. What made it all much more painful, was that his father, who'd loved Cecilia with the passion of youth, was never the same afterwards. The pain Cecilia's leaving inflicted on Enzo absorbed him entirely. He was incapable of sustaining any relationship with his young son. Instead, Luca was packed off to boarding school. There, rumors first reached him that Cecilia had run away with a wealthy shipping magnate who could afford her the lifestyle she'd supposedly always craved. In time, the rumors turned to 'truths' even in Luca's mind.

How could it not affect his view of women? If Cecilia could leave Enzo whom she'd professed to be her forever soul mate, and Luca whom she'd called her little prince, what woman would stay? How could he trust anyone to stay with him when there would always be someone else who might offer more?

But he'd confided in Naomi he was relieved she was so different, sincere and loyal. Despite Luca's fears, he'd dared to hope for something better when he'd realized Naomi was his forever soul mate. She'd felt comforted knowing his heart had broken for her when it became clear her beloved Auntie Elsa was at death's door.

But who could blame him when it became too much to be told the truth about his birth at Auntie Elsa's deathbed? Auntie Elsa's imminent death had spurred on Santina to tell him the truth, finally. At first, he couldn't believe Santina would love Cecilia so much she'd give her the child Cecilia could never have and yearned for so much? That he'd turned out to be that child, had nearly undone him. Were Santina and Enzo's noble words just a facade behind which to hide their sordid affair?

Yes, Naomi could see how easily it could've gone wrong. Luca was beside himself, raging, blaming Enzo and Santina for Cecilia's absence. How could Cecilia have stayed, knowing of their affair, and a child – he – had been the result?

While he'd been ranting, it became clear to Naomi that Luca was still thinking of Cecilia as his mother. Who could blame him? In his mind, Cecilia had always been his mother. He hadn't known another. But when Naomi pointed out to him that Cecilia had never been his mother, that Santina hadn't only given birth to him but she'd always been there for him, only then, did realization finally enter his overwrought mind. Only then, could he forgive them all. But the best news was that through the telling of their story, Enzo and Santina were freed to marry. They finally became Luca's parents united. No one could've hoped for a better outcome.

Naomi's smile reflected how much she'd grown to love Santina.

"Do we have time for our swim today?"

Santina checked her watch.

"Let's go check if everything's ready for the party, first. Enzo's birthday feels different this year."

Santina's smile betrayed her pride.

"I guess it's because it's the first time I'll be attending it as his wife, even though I've celebrated it with him every year since I first met him."

Naomi nodded.

"I'm sure it feels completely different. I'm just so glad you're married now, and Luca knows you're his mum. I don't think I'll ever forget how much it affected him when the woman he thought of as his mother had left. Thank God, you've always been there for him. And now he can honor you as his mother who gave him life. There has been such a change in him since you told him Cecilia wasn't his birth mother but you are."

Santina squeezed Naomi's shoulders.

"You're far too modest, Naomi. Luca told me how you helped him to see the truth. Much of his acceptance of what happened is down to you. And I would never have had the courage to tell Luca the truth if it wasn't for my dear friend, and your adoptive mother, Elsa. I'll never forget what she's done for all of us."

While they'd been talking, Naomi had picked up her handbag and keys.

"I could never repay Auntie Elsa for all she's done for me, either. She'll always live in my heart. And the first thing I'll do when Luca and I return to Desert Lodge is to visit her grave. I cannot believe there are only two months left before we leave for Namibia."

Santina touched Naomi's arm.

"Will you put some flowers on her grave for me, too?"

"Of course. I'm sure Auntie Elsa would love flowers from you, Santina. I can't tell you how thankful I am the two of you became such close friends and you were there for her when she needed a friend such as you. I know you miss her, too."

Naomi held open the double doors for Santina to exit first before she locked it. The two women got into the Armati supercar Luca had given Naomi as a gift. But she didn't have the confidence to drive as fast as Luca usually did and took the corners rather more sedately than the car could go.

Santina had chosen the large restaurant near the Armati headquarters to host Enzo's birthday party. Ristorante La Luna was the Armati team's usual venue for meals and meetings away from the office. As it was within walking distance from the office, people could pop back to the office when they needed to. The party was sure to continue into the early morning hours and it usually interfered with the workaholics' schedules at Armati. This was the perfect solution.

Naomi followed Santina into the restaurant. But she stopped dead in her tracks in the doorway. Luigi and his staff had completely transformed the restaurant into a tropical garden. Naomi had met Luigi once a week and loved how gregarious and flamboyant he was, the total opposite of Enzo, his childhood friend. But it was obvious the two had remained close throughout their lives. Luigi shared his Ristorante La Luna and his passion for gardening with Enzo. Fierce gardening rivals, Luigi agreed wholeheartedly that Enzo's gorgeous home boasted the most beautiful garden Naomi had ever seen. It was the reason Santina had sold her modest home and moved into Enzo's castle after she and Enzo got married. He couldn't bear to part from the garden he'd spent years and a fortune creating, and Santina had always loved it, so it was an easy decision for them.

Naomi still couldn't believe the castle she first saw when Luca drove her home to Modena, belonged to Enzo. It was exactly what she'd always imagined a castle to look like.

Naomi left Santina talking to Luigi and made her way to the toilet at the back of the restaurant. Here, Luigi had placed large potted palm trees and lined the area between the mirrors and the wash basins with mosses and tiny pink flowers. It transformed the usually stylish bathroom into an oasis of serenity.

Just as Naomi closed the door to the cubicle, she heard the bathroom door opening. She could make out the voices of two women, chatting and laughing, friends obviously. But as she listened, not only was she astonished to realize she could understand what they were saying, but their words weren't what she'd expected to hear.

"Well, I still don't get what he sees in that little desert mouse," Voice One said. "She's so plain. So unlike who I thought he'd end up with, you know?"

"I know exactly what you mean," Voice Two said. "She doesn't even speak the language."

The women laughed, and Naomi got the impression they weren't referring to a language that consisted of words.

"Do you remember the last party at his house?" Voice Two asked.

Voice One's response was delayed and sounded muffled, indicating she was applying lipstick.

"Hmm, how can I forget? I'm sure that party was the reason I got to be his secretary when Santina left."

She almost purred as the words left her mouth.

"If only all interviews were so interesting and exciting. I'm still waiting for the de-brief if you know what I mean?"

The women laughed again.

"Don't give up," Voice Two said. "He'll soon tire of her and then there you'll be, ready for your de-brief and whatever else might follow."

"I know, and I agree," Voice One said. "It can't come soon enough. Just imagine…living in that villa, having all that money, having him… And it's not for lack of trying. It wasn't easy to find the drugs and when you get them from the internet, you never know if they're real, do you? But whatever they were, they worked better than I could've imagined."

The women's callous laughter clamped a fist around Naomi's heart.

Voice One snorted as she came to the end of her laughing fit and simultaneously tried to speak.

"By the way, do you like this new top? I got it specially…"

Their voices faded as they left the bathroom and the door shut behind them.

Naomi stood rooted to the spot. She felt as though someone had poured a bucket of ice water over her after punching her in the solar plexus. An immediate headache threatened behind the tears that stung her eyes.

CHAPTER 2

*N*aomi knew she had to move. She couldn't stay in the bathroom for the rest of the afternoon. She had to go home and get ready to attend Enzo's party. She prayed Santina had finished checking everything with Luigi and they could leave as soon as she could get out of the bathroom.

Naomi couldn't even think of going swimming now. Perhaps she'd never be able to go to the Armati pool again. That these women might have been watching her swimming there was too horrible to contemplate. No, Luca had promised to instal a swimming pool at their home, and she'd hold him to it, instead.

Luca. Of course, Luca had a life before her.

Naomi had always known he must've been popular with the ladies. He was beyond good-looking, his presence a shiny thing impossible to ignore and he had the money to be attractive to many gold-diggers. His name and money carried the prestige of something akin to a fairy tale. Hadn't she felt that way herself since meeting him, that she'd been living in a dream from which she'd never wanted to awake? But for her, it wasn't about the money. It was all about him. He was her soul mate, wasn't he? She couldn't let him down. Not tonight. The importance of her first company outing hadn't escaped her. Yes, she'd met some of Luca's colleagues and employees. But tonight's event would be the first time everyone would see her in her role as Luca's wife, and Enzo and Santina's daughter-in-law.

Although Luca had said nothing, Naomi had the feeling he felt as trepidatious about the event as she did. When Santina had taken her dress shopping, Luca had handed over his personal credit card and told her to buy whatever she wanted. He'd emphasized she didn't need to think about the cost of the dress as his card would cover whatever she bought. He'd arranged for Enzo's chauffeur to take them to Bologna.

That day had been warm and smelled like summer. Bologna was smaller than Naomi had remembered from her first time there with Luca. But Santina knew where all the best shops were, and they'd spent a few pleasant hours going from one boutique to the next, trying on dresses and accessories. Finally, and with Santina's help, Naomi had chosen a figure-hugging red dress with an eye-watering price tag. The shop assistants had fawned over her and confirmed Naomi looked like a goddess in the dress. In truth, it was how she'd felt when she'd tried it on. With the same superstition that befits a wedding dress, Naomi had kept Luca from seeing the dress until the event.

Buoyed by these memories, Naomi felt less mousy than Luca's secretary and the friend had described her earlier. It gave her the courage to leave the bathroom. There were fewer people in the restaurant now. She immediately saw Santina sitting at a table by herself, a glass of water in front of her.

Santina looked up as Naomi walked towards her.

"Ah, there you are. Are you okay?"

Santina's eyes were full of concern, but she visibly relaxed when Naomi nodded.

"Yes, sorry. I think I was a little longer than I'd intended. I was admiring the great job Luigi's staff had made of the bathroom. It's completely transformed."

Santina looked around the room and nodded.

"He has done a great job. I'm sure Enzo will love it.

Santina got up.

"We should probably get going. I have made an appointment for us both with my hairdresser. If you don't mind, come to the castle?"

With the words she'd heard in the ladies' room still in her head, Naomi gratefully followed Santina out of the restaurant and back to her car. She wouldn't allow anything to spoil tonight. Perhaps everything would be okay. She had the killer dress, and soon she'd have the hair to go with it.

Santina must've sensed something.

She put a hand on Naomi's arm.

"It's a first for us both. We are now the Armati women. Something to be proud of, si?"

An hour later, when Naomi pulled up to her own home, she felt much calmer and more hopeful. Santina's hairdresser had done a great job on her hair. A few loosened tendrils softened the up-do. It was perfect for the strappy dress's stylish cowl neckline and the gold shoes and accessories she'd bought specially.

She'd expected Luca to come home at some point to have a shower and get ready. But fifteen minutes before Santina's arrival so they could go to the party together, Luca still hadn't turned up. Nor had he responded to her text and call. He had to be busy, she knew, and would respond later when he could. She knew he kept clean clothes in his office and could use the facilities there to have a shower and freshen up.

No wonder Santina had insisted on taking him on the vacation that led him to Namibia and the meeting that was to change both their lives forever. Luca worked long hours, and before she came on the scene, Naomi suspected he must've spent most of his time at his office. But who could blame him? Armati was a family concern, and once Enzo retired, all would rest on Luca's shoulders.

Naomi got her handbag and keys ready when she heard Santina's car drive up. Quickly, Naomi went to open the door for her. Santina looked impeccable as always in a stylish and elegant deep-blue pants suit as she walked inside.

"Oh, you look like a dream, Naomi. Luca will love you in that dress. Very much the Armati leading lady."

Naomi smiled.

"Speak for yourself, dear Santina. At least in the dress department, I feel we'll outshine just about everyone there."

At the restaurant, as though he'd been watching out for them, Enzo saw them the moment they walked through the door and came to welcome them at once. Waiters with silver trays offered drinks, and Enzo steered them towards a large round table at the center of the restaurant. Many of his colleagues and their wives already sat at the table. But there was still no sign of Luca.

As though Enzo could read Naomi's thoughts, he took her elbow and leaned towards her so she could hear his voice above the cacophony in the room.

"Luca will be here soon. He's just doing something I've asked him to finish. I hope you don't mind?"

How could she mind?

Still, Naomi felt grateful for Enzo and Santina's reassuring presence. Everyone seemed to be talking simultaneously in their typical passionate Italian way. Together with the music, the noise was deafening and overwhelming. They spoke too fast, and Naomi couldn't follow any of the conversations.

She attracted rather more attention than she would've liked, but no one approached her directly. Perhaps their reticence was because she was sitting beside Enzo? He exuded an air of austerity which all but his closest colleagues and friends disregarded. Naomi was aware of curious looks and stares in her direction and no doubt, opinions offered. Did all these people perceive her as a desert mouse, like Luca's secretary and friend did? Surely not. Surely, those women were harsh only because they were jealous.

Luca suddenly stood behind her and placed his hands over her eyes.

She knew it was him before he said, "Guess who?"

She pulled his hands from her eyes and kissed them, leaving red lipstick marks on the backs of both. He leaned over her and kissed her forehead, her nose and lightly touched her lips with his. Then, he slid into the seat beside her. On his other side, Naomi noticed a stunning young woman taking her seat.

Luca leaned slightly back in his seat and indicated with his hand before speaking.

"Have you met my new secretary?"

Luca gestured to the young woman beside him.

"This is Fia."

Fia's dark eyes carried superiority and disdain when they met Naomi's.

CHAPTER 3

$\mathcal{L}$uca had barely sat down before he leaned into Naomi's neck.

"You look good enough to eat, Mrs Armati."

He nipped her earlobe between his teeth and bit down lightly.

She could feel him smile at her gasp. The warmth of his body and the vitality of his presence immediately made her feel as though all was right in the world.

"Will you stay right here? I just have to check something with Luigi quickly."

Luca stroked down her shoulder towards her breast as he stood up, his hand hot and promising and making her shiver with desire.

"I won't be long, okay?"

She nodded, and he kissed her forehead before he went looking for Luigi. His absence left Naomi feeling as though she was suddenly sitting in a cold, dark room. She shook her head, feeling silly. He'd be back soon.

Fia's voice was suddenly near and very clear.

"Your hair looks great. Is it your own?"

It took Naomi a moment to process Fia's words. But then she

remembered Fia was Italian. Maybe something got lost in translation. She couldn't possibly have meant to be that rude, could she?

Instead, Naomi smiled at her.

"Thank you for the compliment. But I'm not sure I understand what you mean?"

Fia sighed in exasperation at the stupidity she had to deal with.

She tilted her head and shook her long dark hair before speaking again, slowly, emphasizing her words as though she was speaking to a toddler.

"I mean, is it your own hair, or did you have extensions put in and color?"

Again, Naomi wondered if this was just the Italian way to be so direct.

"I see. No, it is all my own hair. No color and no extensions."

Fia sat back in her chair, and Naomi could have sworn she heard Fia say, "So you say."

The chair beside her suddenly moved back, and Santina sat down beside Naomi, her warm smile a welcome sight.

"You girls seem to discuss something interesting. I was curious so thought I'd join you. Everyone else is talking shop."

Fia lent forward and twisted her body so she could take in both Santina and Naomi.

A lovely smile lit up her face.

"I was just complimenting Naomi on her hair."

Santina lifted an eyebrow.

"Oh, I didn't know you two were on a first name basis already. I thought Luca had only just introduced you?"

Fia's face flushed pink, and she stumbled over her words.

"I…yes, I… I meant to say, Mrs Armati. I was complimenting Mrs Armati on her hair."

Santina frowned and squinted at Fia.

"I hope so. I thought I heard something different."

Fia was squirming in her seat but sending eye daggers at Naomi as though it was Naomi's fault she'd come under Santina's fire. But Santina was waving and smiling at someone across the table and didn't notice. Or so Naomi thought until Santina suddenly turned back to Fia.

"This table has been reserved for the executives, Fia. Perhaps you could find the table where you are supposed to be before dinner is served?"

Naomi thought Fia might explode, but she had to give the girl credit for keeping her voice level.

Again, Fia shook her hair before speaking.

"But Luca - "

"Luca would agree with me." Santina interrupted.

Naomi wondered how old Fia was, as she watched the girl chew her lip, got up and with a "fine," stomp off to find her dining companions.

Santina turned to Naomi.

"I'm sorry you had to be subjected to her tantrums, Naomi. You don't deserve it. But I'm sure I don't have to explain to you all these young girls have spent their days vying for Luca's attention. Your appearance was a shock to them, I'm sure. You can imagine the prestige attached to working directly for Luca, si? Until now, he had some protection from them because I was his secretary. But now that I'm no longer working for him, he's at their mercy."

Naomi found it difficult to hide her astonishment at Santina's perceptiveness.

She blew out a breath and touched the back of Santina's hand.

"Thank you so much, Santina. I thought I was just being silly."

Santina patted Naomi's hand.

"You most certainly were not being silly. I'd noticed Fia and another girl following you to the bathroom when we were here this afternoon. Knowing how these girls operate, you didn't have to tell me they'd said something unpleasant about you in there. I had hoped you wouldn't understand their words, but your face said it all when you came out."

Naomi didn't know how to express her gratitude to this amazing lady who was now her mother-in-law. In her heart and mind, Santina had already begun to live in the place in her life her beloved Auntie Elsa had always occupied. Santina had the same warmth and caring heart Auntie Elsa had. Not that anyone could ever replace Auntie Elsa and Naomi still missed her every day. But whenever she became too sad, she tried to remember Auntie Elsa was now with Uncle Wouter, her husband and soul mate, who'd died many years ago.

Before Naomi could respond, Santina continued.

"I have never seen Luca as happy as he's been since meeting you, Naomi. I won't allow anything to mar his happiness if I can help it. I'll talk to him and see what can be done about Fia."

"Oh, please. Not on my account. I don't want to be the reason she loses her job."

At that moment, Luca slid into the chair next to Naomi.

"Who's losing their job? I just heard the end of that conversation."

Santina leaned forward and smiled past Naomi at her son.

"No one needs to lose their job, darling. But I do think you need to find Fia another position, don't you?"

Luca's face was a study in confusion. He looked from Santina to Naomi and back again.

"What happened? Where is she?"

Santina turned to thank the waitress who'd delivered her starter before she responded to Luca.

"I asked her to find the table where her colleagues are sitting."

Luca nodded his thanks to the waitress delivering the starters before turning back to Santina.

"Why?"

Santina was smiling at her son.

"Don't be dense, darling. Why do you think?"

She nodded slightly in Naomi's direction.

A lightbulb went off in Luca's eyes.

"Oh, I see. Oh, God, amore mio, I'm so sorry. It never occurred to me there might be -"

Naomi placed a hand on Luca's arm.

"No, please. It's nothing. She was a little rude, but it's understandable, I guess."

Luca looked around, evidently for Fia.

Naomi put both hands on his arm to make him stay.

"It's okay, Luca. Really."

"No, it's not, amore mio. I never, ever want you to feel uncomfortable because of some jealous female. Don't worry. I'll move her to another department tomorrow."

"But it would mean a demotion?"

"I'll find a way and make it worth her while. I won't have anything or anyone making problems for you, for us."

Naomi could see Luca had made up his mind. Nothing she said would make him change it, now.

Instead, she smiled.

"Well, if you really think it's necessary."

Luca turned his body fully towards her and gently put his hands on either side of her face.

"Mrs Armati, I love you. I've never been happier in my life. I know what these women are like. I have radar for them, and I can kick myself for not noticing Fia's attitude sooner. But I was so busy. Can you forgive me?"

Naomi slid her hands down Luca's arms. She could see how tired he was. The dark circles under his eyes and his new, thinner frame told of hours spent working and not looking after himself. Once whatever deadlines he was working on were over, she'd make sure he got enough rest, exercised and ate properly again.

"I appreciate you taking care of us so well, my Luca. There is nothing to forgive. You couldn't have known -"

"Yes, I could. I should've seen it. Remember what we talked

about that day in the truck when we were caught in the storm in the desert?"

Naomi nodded.

She remembered how Luca had misinterpreted a conversation she'd had with her friend, Kerri. That day in the desert, Luca had told her how often he'd heard women talking about how they'd wanted to be with him because of his money. Overhearing Naomi and Kerri's conversation had almost led to a total withdrawal from Naomi even though he loved her deeply.

Naomi still found it difficult to believe any woman would want to be with him only for his money or for the prestige of being with the heir to the Armati supercar dynasty. Luca was so beautiful inside and out. His spirit shone through his whole body. He was kind and generous and loving. More than that, he was her soul mate.

Luca was watching Naomi intently and appeared to follow her thoughts as she was thinking them.

A smile curled around his lips.

"I'm still so grateful for that storm, amore mio."

"As am I, my Luca."

A giggle escaped Naomi. In her mind's eye, she saw Luca's struggle again to get down on one knee in the confines of the truck to ask for her hand in marriage.

He took her hand and chuckled as the same image flashed across his mind's eye.

CHAPTER 4

*N*aomi yawned and stretched and reached out her hand out to the other side of the bed. It was empty.

She sat up. The red neon numbers on the alarm read nine twenty-two. She yawned again and tied her hair with a scrunchie she took from her bedside table.

Luca was a machine or a God. Naomi had good evidence he wasn't a machine. But no one alive would dispute he was a God. At least she thought so. He looked like one and behaved like one. The good kind. But even a God couldn't possibly get up this early for work. Not when they'd stayed at Enzo's birthday party until nearly two o'clock in the morning. But despite the late hour when they'd got home, sleep was the last thing on either of their minds. Naomi worked out their vigorous lovemaking had to have lasted for at least another two hours. It meant Luca had less than four hours sleep. He had to be exhausted today, or at least more exhausted than he'd been looking lately.

Naomi laid back against her pillows, picked up Luca's pillow and inhaled the smell of him. In her mind's eye, she could still feel his body on hers and his clever hands. Hands that knew exactly where to touch her. Such pleasure followed her arousal to the point where she couldn't think clearly, where everything became sensation only, and touch, smell, taste. Now, they were married, and she felt completely safe with him, she took part in their lovemaking with as much enthusiasm and vigor as he did. He was her everything. Just the thought of more such pleasure with him stirred her desire again. She had to press her hand against herself to suppress the pressure building. What was he doing to her? She was becoming as insatiable as he seemed to be. It helped that they loved each other so much.

Naomi picked up her phone and typed a quick message.

Hope you're not too tired, today, Mr Armati? I know just how to relax you when you get home. xxx

Send.

She giggled when moments later her phone buzzed with a message from him.

God Mrs Armati how can I get through this day faster??? Can you wear your black negligee and stockings when I get home? Can't WAIT to see you!!! xxx

Sure Mr Amati. Your wish is my command. I'll be waiting for you. Have an awesome day at the office. xxx

Send.

Immediately her phone buzzed again.

You tease! Groan.

xxx

Naomi allowed herself one last stretch before getting up. She could hear Signora Giana in the kitchen. It was a good thing they'd kept her on. She was an amazing cook, and she kept the rest of the staff on a tight rein. Naomi agreed when Luca said he didn't feel they could let her go after she'd been with him forever. It meant the villa, and everything that entailed running it, would be one less thing for Naomi to worry about and she was grateful for that. It was enough to deal with being in a different county and culture and a newlywed. And now she'd inherited Desert Lodge from Auntie Elsa, she intended to be as hands-on about the running of the lodge as Luca had predicted she'd want to be.

But thank God for Kerri. Not only was it great they were best friends because it made communication so much easier, but Kerri was also the best manager they'd ever had at the lodge. Naomi was grateful Auntie Elsa had thought so, too. Kerri's presence at Desert Lodge had made it easier for Naomi to agree when Luca had suggested they spend six months in Italy and six months in Namibia. Naomi wasn't so sure about the six months in Namibia. How would Luca cope? The man was a workaholic. But he too had good people in place here at the Armati headquarters. They'd have to see how it goes.

She threw on her caftan and floated downstairs where the aroma of freshly brewed coffee met her halfway and propelled her towards the kitchen.

Signora Giana greeted Naomi with a broad smile and placed a mug of delicious coffee in front of Naomi on the kitchen table. A bowl of muesli and yoghurt soon followed.

Signora Giana was a marvel. Naomi still applauded the woman for her willingness to learn so quickly what Naomi's favorite meals were even when the Signora clearly regarded Naomi's eating habits eccentric. It didn't take Naomi long to understand Signora Giana had decided to indulge Luca's foreign bride good-heartedly. She presented Naomi with everything she'd wanted but never quite in the right way as though something between her intensions and the practical went amiss.

But Naomi loved this time of the day when she could enjoy her breakfast and listen to Signora Giana's stories. The older lady sat down opposite Naomi and took small sips of her coffee while regaling Naomi with the local gossip. She spoke mostly Italian, but Naomi managed to follow nearly all her stories.

Who'd have guessed the sleepy rural hills around Modena harbored such goings-on?

Naomi wondered if the tales were just figments of Signora

Giana's fertile imagination. Surely, there couldn't be that many affairs and scandals? It sounded like a soap opera. But Naomi listened and nodded and laughed when Signora Giana did.

After breakfast, Naomi went to work. The smaller bedroom near the front of the house which she'd turned into her office was the perfect space away from the rest of the house to work. Large windows meant lovely bright sunshine in the mornings especially.

As Italy was an hour ahead of Namibia, Naomi went through her correspondence and responded to emails, made notes on what she wanted to discuss with Kerri, and wrestled with whatever problems they currently faced. There weren't many because Kerri was such a good manager. But both women had wanted to expand Desert Lodge, and they loved to brainstorm to see which ideas were best.

Kerri's suggestion to have specially designed Armati dune buggies available to Desert Lodge guests exclusively, had been inspired. News had traveled fast, and it was satisfying that so many young 'princes' and 'princesses,' went there to enjoy taking one of the sought-after buggies for a spin in the desert. It helped that the dunes near Desert Lodge were some of the highest in the Namib Desert and made for fantastic and heart-stopping experiences.

Naomi and Kerri had been thinking of something equally appealing to add to the arsenal of goodies to offer their other guests. Not everyone who visited the lodge wanted to spend their vacation being quite so active. But good, workable ideas seemed more difficult to generate.

An hour later, Naomi was still thinking and making notes when Skype on her computer rang. Kerri had evidently arrived at her office at Desert Lodge and was ready to chat.

"That bitch."

Naomi had expected no other reaction from Kerri when she'd

finished her story about what had happened with Fia the day before.

The red blooms on Kerri's cheeks were ample evidence of her annoyance on Naomi's behalf.

"Wait till I get a hold of her."

Naomi smiled at her friend.

"I'm almost feeling sorry for her. Just as well you'll never meet her."

Kerri did that thing she always did when she was bursting to tell a secret of her own.

"Well, about that... You know Johan had already asked me to marry him? We were thinking of doing it this fall and then coming to Italy for our honeymoon."

Naomi gasped.

When she spoke, her disappointment was clear in her voice.

"But that's when we were planning on being at Desert Lodge. It means we'll miss you when you're here."

Kerri frowned.

"I know. But is your coming here then cast in stone? It'll be quite difficult for us to change all the wedding plans. We're flying to his family in Johannesburg. It's all set up already."

Naomi leaned back in her chair and ran her hands through her hair, undoing the scrunchie.

"I see. Well, no, our plans aren't set in stone. I'm sure Luca would be more than happy to stay here a little longer, especially since he's knee-deep in some big projects at the moment. But that means we'll miss your wedding. You'll just have to have a ceremony in Italy, too. You realize there are four of us here who would like to celebrate with you."

"Aw, hun, that's so lovely. I don't see why we can't have a cere-mony there with all of you guys. It'll be so romantic. But we'll be thoroughly married as people at Desert Lodge want us to have a ceremony here. They can't all go to Jo'burg."

Naomi laughed.

"Well, I don't see a problem with three weddings. It's a great thing to celebrate, and you and Johan are so perfect together. That's why everyone wants to share in your joy."

Kerri's eyes brimmed with unshed tears.

"What a lovely thing to say. I'll call Johan and tell him when we've finished."

"Hmm…with both of us in Modena, we must make very good arrangements at the lodge so nothing crazy happens there while we're both gallivanting in Italy."

It was Kerri's turn to smile.

"Don't you worry. I'll make sure we have the best cover for that time."

Her smile broadened until it stretched over her whole face.

"It's so exciting to think I'll be with you soon. I can't wait to see where you live now, what your life is like…"

Kerri's eyes narrowed.

"And Fia… I'd like to meet Fia."

Naomi briefly wondered if she should feel sorry for Fia, but couldn't help the giggle that bubbled up from her stomach. Evidently, Kerri thought it was hilarious, too.

When they could both finally talk again and had wiped the laughter tears from their eyes, they said their goodbyes and promised to action the tasks they'd set for themselves.

Naomi stayed staring at the computer screen for moments after Kerri's face had disappeared.

Although it was lovely that Santina had come to her rescue, it may have inflamed Fia's dislike of her even more. Naomi was under no illusions about what the other woman could get up to. Fia was on her home territory, after all, with everything in her favor. Well, perhaps not everything.

A secret smile formed on Naomi's lips.

It may be time to recall all she'd learned about survival from the San people of the desert.

CHAPTER 5

*W*hen the alarm on her phone went off at six thirty, Naomi closed her office door behind her and headed for the shower. She wanted to be fresh and fabulous for Luca when he got home.

En route, she checked the dinner situation. Signora Giana was a godsend. Naomi was used to Chef at Desert Lodge creating African culinary masterpieces to wow the guests, but Signora Giana's fares were wonderfully Italian. She'd left a delicious pasta dish in the oven, and a large salad rested in a sealed container in the fridge. A bottle of white wine from the Armati vineyard nestled next to the salad.

In the dining room, two place settings sat beside each other at the top of the long marble table. Delicate wine glasses complemented the silver cutlery bearing the Armati family crest. Flowers and candles decorated the table and the fireplace on the wall behind it.

On the other side of the room, Signora Giana had opened the floor-to-ceiling curtains and a window. The soft fragrance of the roses in the garden wafted through the open window, an immediate reminder of the gorgeous rose arch under which they'd got married.

In her mind's eye, Naomi saw Auntie Elsa's rose garden which had provided the many roses in Naomi's bouquet and those for the arch that had been constructed in the desert. But it also reminded of the sadness that Auntie Elsa was no longer here. Memories of her beloved adoptive mother occupied her mind as she ambled up the staircase to get ready for Luca.

After her shower, Naomi paid meticulous attention to her makeup. Just because she almost never wore any, didn't mean she didn't know how to apply it. But she preferred to keep it subtle even as she wanted her makeup to complement what she was wearing. She'd dressed in the outfit Luca had asked for in his text message. Over her black negligee, she wore a floaty floral chiffon robe. It fell to the floor, hiding her outfit. It would be no fun to reveal the after-dinner surprise too soon.

She'd just sprayed on the musky rose perfume Luca had bought her in Venice when she heard the front door opened and shut.

The familiar sound of his keys on the marble table in the foyer followed his voice as he called to her.

"Honey, I'm home."

Naomi smiled.

Within months, her entire life had changed. She didn't even recognize who she now was. But she felt as though she'd come home, that she finally belonged, and she loved it all.

Dinner, as usual, became the foreplay to their lovemaking. Luca often interrupted eating mouthfuls of the delicious pasta to kiss Naomi and fondle her breasts through her robe. As his playfulness increased, so did her giggling.

If she hadn't known better, she'd never have guessed he was the heir apparent to the Armati supercar dynasty, and she was now the owner of a large safari lodge in Namibia. But she couldn't deny the fun as they continued to behave like teenagers.

It wouldn't last as their life together grew, and developed, she knew. She only hoped they'd always keep this element of fun, and their connection would develop into the kind her beloved Auntie Elsa and Uncle Wouter shared. Those two were soul mates in every way, and that's how Naomi felt about Luca, too.

Naomi made a mental note to eat before her husband came home in the future. He seemed to inhale his food, ready to satisfy his more carnal appetites. Tonight, was no exception. Luca had barely finished his last mouthful of pasta before he grabbed her hand and with a wink and a twinkle in his eye, led her up the stairs to their bedroom.

Once there, Luca excused himself and moments later, the shower come on. His lovely baritone voice floated through the door as he sang some Italian love song, no doubt for Naomi's benefit. But she could hardly contain her giggles as the buzzing of his sonic toothbrush periodically interrupted his singing. Was he doing everything at once?

She visited her bathroom next to his, to brush her teeth and check her makeup one last time. Experience had taught her it wouldn't stay on for long after Luca came out of the bathroom. As if to support her suspicion, Luca was naked and still damp from the shower when he pushed her down on their bed.

His kisses started gentle, and grew passionate and deep, his tongue doing things to her she could never have dreamed of. His were kisses for drowning in. There was no coming up for air, nor did she want to. His hands were everywhere, touching, stroking, probing. Such clever hands. He knew just where to touch to arouse her to the point she craved him inside her with a fierceness that surprised even her. But he wasn't ready to let her enjoy release that way yet. Instead, he kissed all the way down her body, caressing her, spreading her legs as he went. The self-consciousness that sometimes still afflicted her at his boldness, evaporated as he laid one hand flat on her stomach while the other opened her up to him, claiming her completely.

His eyes were dark with passion when he looked up, his voice husky with desire.

"I want to please you, my Naomi."

He didn't wait to see her small nod, but when his tongue touched her, she couldn't hold back the groan that escaped her lips. Her body arched as she pushed harder against his insistent mouth. Sooner than she could imagine, wave after wave of pleasure flooded through her body.

Satisfied she felt fulfilled, Luca, clearly unable to wait any longer, entered her with one swift stroke. Both gasped. Luca's thrusts brought Naomi to ecstasy over and over until she didn't know where one orgasm finished and the next one began. She could feel him stop now and then and knew it wasn't because he was tired. Rather, he wanted to prolong their lovemaking for as long as he could.

"I'm so turned-on, amore. I don't think I can last much longer."

"Then, come when you want to, my love."

She loved watching his face as he poured himself into her. But it was a good thing she was using contraceptives. She wanted to enjoy their life together first before thoughts of babies became an issue. Was she selfish? As Luca hadn't raised the issue either, she didn't think so.

As their breathing returned to normal along with their heartbeats, they lay entangled, legs and arms intertwined, sweaty and happy.

Luca shifted and pulled Naomi into his chest as he stroked her hair.

"So, what have you been up to today, Mrs Armati?"

Naomi told him about Kerri and Johan's wedding plans and the idea to have another blessing for them here when they came to Italy.

As she talked, he nodded in agreement.

"We could do something lovely for them. I really like Johan. And Kerri, too. We could even do it here?"

Naomi leaned in to kiss him.

"That will be perfect Mr Armati. I'd love it."

He returned her kiss, his lips lingering on hers while he spoke.

"Then, Mrs Armati, it's done. I'll get Anna to arrange a wedding organizer tomorrow."

"Who is Anna?"

"My new secretary. I told you I was going to move Fia elsewhere. That happened today. She didn't seem unhappy, and Anna is a far better secretary, anyway, so I'm happy, too."

"I see. I'm really glad I wasn't the cause of Fia losing her job."

"You're far too kind, Mrs Armati."

"You feel the same, don't you?"

Luca laughed.

"Perhaps not. I'm far more ruthless in business than you can imagine."

"No, actually… I can imagine it. I suspected it ever since I met you."

"How so, Mrs Armati? Did I give the game away so easily?"

She kissed his nose.

"No, Mr Armati. But the way you swim told me more about you than you could imagine."

Luca laughed again. It was such a lovely sound.

"Touche."

Naomi moved away from him and leaned on her elbow.

"Oh, and you'll never guess... I've been writing down the stories Signora Giana has been telling me. I wrote them just as exercises for my lessons, but Francisca says they're good enough to publish."

Luca pulled her down and covered her face with kisses.

"That's wonderful, Mrs Armati. And high praise, indeed, coming from Francisca."

"Yes, I thought so, too."

"But what?"

Naomi rolled her bottom lip against her teeth.

"Well, they're not my stories, are they? I'd feel weird publishing them when they belong to Signora Giana."

Luca lifted a strand of hair from Naomi's face and kissed her again.

"Did you write them?"

"Yes."

Luca kissed her breasts, gently biting her nipples which made her gasp and yearn for him once more.

"Then they're yours."

She ran her fingers through his hair as his head rested on her chest.

"I don't know... It just feels wrong."

"Have you spoken to Signora Giana about it?"

"No. But I will. Tomorrow."

Luca wriggled against her. Naomi could feel him getting harder on her leg. After a few moments of kissing with more ardor, he spoke. She knew that voice.

"Mrs Armati?"

"Yes, Mr Armati?"

"Do you think we could get back to more important matters?"

CHAPTER 6

*L*uca stood looking at Naomi's sleeping form as he buttoned up his shirt. He felt surprisingly alert and awake. The veil of sluggish exhaustion that had fogged his brain over the last few months seemed to have lifted, and now everything appeared clearer and more vivid once again.

His eyes traveled over his wife's face. She was becoming more beautiful each day. Not that she wasn't before, but she seemed to have grown into herself. That's all he could think might have caused the transformation in the gorgeous young woman he'd met in Namibia less than six months ago.

Hers wasn't the beauty that belonged to the models he had to work with, but to him, she was more beautiful than any model could ever be. Her beauty had a depth to it, a solidity, earthiness. It was real, not some illusion. His desert goddess was fragile and strong simultaneously. Her physical presence, like her spirit, revealed an honest vulnerability that could never be hidden.

That he was blessed to find such an angel in such an apparently desolate place, seemed incomprehensible. Yet, here she was. In his home, in his bed. In their home, their bed. His wife. She was the epitome of the vitality and unearthly beauty that existed in the desert she loved so much and which he'd come to appreciate nearly as much as she did.

Now, her face wore the appearance of deep contentment. It mirrored how he felt. He couldn't remember ever being happier than he'd been these past few months with Naomi. She was everything he'd ever wanted, and so much more.

As he bent down to kiss her lightly, he lifted her soft blonde hair from her face. She moved in her sleep, and her unique scent reached him. It was something he'd never noticed with other women before. Yes, they all wore perfume, but Naomi's fragrance was a mixture of perfume and underneath, her very own smell. It reminded him of his favorite aromas all rolled into one, like freshly baked bread, or the smell of coffee in the morning, toast even, the way the air smelled just before it rained in summer and the earthier smell of freshly cut grass.

Her smell did things to him. God, what was wrong with him? He wanted her all the time, sometimes so fiercely, it bordered on pain. Is this part of what it felt like to love someone completely? His experiences with other women paled into such insignificance he couldn't remember anyone before Naomi.

Luca touched his arousal to relieve the pressure. He could hardly wait until he saw her again tonight. Instead, he picked up his jacket and waited several minutes for his diminishing passion to allow him to walk down the corridor comfortably. He descended the staircase, careful not to make a noise. Gently, he closed the front door behind him.

For a few moments, he stood still on the porch of the home he now shared with Naomi. It had never been a home before. Now, he couldn't think of it as anything else. He took a deep breath, inhaling the fresh morning air that carried notes of the flowers from their garden and the earthiness of the vineyards further away. The sun's first rays and the dawn chorus greeted him with typical exuberance.

It was always difficult for him to leave Naomi, but today he was looking forward to getting to work early. The new project excited him. It was going more smoothly than he could have imagined and it spurred him on to go for bigger projects than they'd attempted before. Maybe this year they'd win Formula One over Ferrari.

As he got into his car, he looked up at his home again as though to make sure it would stay safe until his return. He half hoped Naomi had awoken and was waving to him from a window, but he didn't blame her for being still asleep. It was very early. The thought somehow connected to her excitement about Johan's and Kerri's ceremony here at their home.

Luca made a mental note to talk to Anna about getting a wedding planner on board to arrange everything. It would be both fun and a pleasure to return their kindness. With these thoughts in his mind, he drove down the long driveway. At this time of the morning, there was hardly any traffic, and it would take mere minutes to get to work.

He loved this time of the day when the Armati building was as quiet and desolate as it was going to get all day. Most people were still asleep at this hour. But he liked to get here first and, while having his breakfast, enjoy the stillness of the hour to think about the day ahead and what he wanted to accomplish.

He'd already sketched out the articles he wanted Anna to prepare for social media and newsletters and dictated several letters she needed to get out on his behalf.

He congratulated himself on Anna's appointment. She was well-versed in the company ethos, having worked for Enzo. But Enzo was getting ready to retire and didn't need her full-time services in quite the same way as before. It was a fitting transfer for her and Luca. He'd been delighted when both Enzo and Anna had accepted his proposal that she worked for them both, meanwhile. Not only was she a consummate professional and super-efficient but she also understood Luca's perfectionistic tendencies in this fast-paced, competitive industry.

Luca was thankful all the staff knew his habits well and worked with him to make his life as easy as it could be. It was the only way he could be as effective as he was. He appreciated it. Everyone who worked at Armati played a vital role in its success. He was particularly grateful they'd attracted an excellent chef like Marco to work there. Marco saved him on many a day when he'd worked so late, he'd forgotten to eat and Marco always arrived early to prepare Luca's breakfast before the rest of the staff descended on the well-appointed dining room. Luca never ate in the dining room. Instead, someone always brought his meals up to his office where he ate, sitting at the conference table with a view over the hills.

Luca was just finishing responding to an email when a knock on his door let him know that his breakfast had arrived.

He didn't look up from his keyboard as he responded.

"Avanti."

The door opened, and the sound of footsteps dampened by the plush carpet came towards him. It had to be a new waiter who didn't know where to put the breakfast.

Luca still didn't look up as he wanted to finish his emails before having his breakfast. He wanted time to enjoy his meal without thinking about the items on his immediate admin to-do list.

"Just put the tray on the table. Thank you."

But the footsteps continued coming closer to his desk. Luca was sure he'd given a clear instruction.

He frowned and looked up.

Instead of a waiter, Fia stood in front of his desk. Despite the comfortable temperature in the building, she wore a long buttoned-up coat. It was stylish, but something seemed off about it. Luca couldn't put his finger on it.

He didn't smile when he spoke.

"Morning, Fia. What are you doing here?"

Fia licked her lips and sashayed forward. She ran her hand

along his desk as she walked displaying her long red nails before she ended up next to him.

"I thought I'd check up on my gorgeous boss. I know Anna is working for you now, but let's face it, she's not exactly dynamic, is she?"

Fia leaned towards Luca and stroked a finger down his face, her nose crinkling as she whispered conspiratorially.

"She doesn't know -"

Luca grabbed Fia's wrist and pulled her hand away from his face as he stood up.

"What are you doing?"

He pointed towards the door.

"Get out of my office. Now."

But Fia smiled and ripped open her coat. Luca realized it had a Velcro fastening. She'd evidently been planning this little scene.

Just as Luca went to take her by the arm and lead her forcibly to the door, she dropped the garment. Underneath, she wore a black silk slip, black suspender belt and black stockings.

Fia shook out her long black hair and contemplated Luca, her hand on her hip. This time, when he took her arm, she didn't resist. Instead, she leaned into him as though she was going to kiss him. At that moment, the door burst open and several things happened all at once.

Another one of the young secretaries, no doubt Fia's accomplice, took several pictures of Luca and Fia with her iPhone. Right behind the girl, Anna walked in through the wooden double doors together with Marco, who was carrying a tray with Luca's breakfast.

For seconds, no one said or did anything, and then, all hell broke loose.

Luca never lost his temper, but this was too much, even for someone like him who lived by ethical principles. He quickly picked up Fia's coat, draped it over her shoulders and dragged her towards the door by her arm. When he reached the girl with the phone, he snatched it from her hand and pushed her towards the door. But Anna had reacted equally quickly. She had her phone in her hand and had summoned security. Two tall, burly men in uniforms ran through the door just as Luca finally dragged the reluctant Fia there.

Luca was so angry, he shouted at the security guards.

"Get them out of here and call the police! Don't let them leave!"

The men took hold of a girl each and marched them down the corridor.

Marco, who'd stopped in his tracks, closed his mouth and quickly deposited Luca's breakfast tray on the conference table. He busied himself laying out the place setting for Luca as he, or one of his waiters, did every morning.

If Luca had glanced in Marco's direction, he'd have seen the chef's excited expression at the unexpected events so early in the day but simultaneously also a deep disapproval of Fia's stunt.

Once Marco had finished with the table, he quickly went to leave but Anna motioned for him to wait in her office.

Marco had been only minutes depositing the breakfast, but Luca didn't want to discuss with Anna what had just happened in front of anyone. As far as he was concerned, the fewer people who knew about it, the better.

He was leaning against the wall with one hand, the other pinching the top of his nose, eyes closed, as he waited for Marco to leave.

Anna was still talking to security on her phone as they informed her step by step what was happening downstairs. But she was keeping an eye on Luca. She never doubted that he was entirely innocent. Fia and her kind were unscrupulous young women, predatory in going after what they wanted.

Anna had expected some repercussion after Luca had asked that she replace Fia. But no one, not even her, could have foreseen what she'd witnessed this morning.

Both Enzo and Luca had always been kind to her, as had Santina. Everyone had speculated about who could replace Santina when she'd married Enzo and then retired. But because Enzo had still needed her, Anna never imagined she'd end up working for Luca.

She'd been very concerned about her job as Enzo's retirement neared. She was older than Fia and her cronies, but too young to retire yet. What else would she do? She loved her work at Armati. Being offered the top Personal Assistant job to Luca was a godsend. She felt so grateful. This was her opportunity to repay him for his faith in her.

The moment his office door closed behind Marco, Luca handed Anna the phone he'd confiscated from the girl who'd taken the pictures.

His voice sounded tight from the anger that still coursed through his body.

"The police might want that for evidence. But once they're done with it, please make sure every single picture she took on there, is deleted from the phone, or the cloud, or wherever else it might be stored."

Anna took the phone and nodded.

"I'm sorry this happened to you, Luca."

"Thank you. It never occurred to me Fia would stoop this low. I guess there's a first for everything."

"Yes, I didn't expect this either. But I knew she might try to do something."

Luca walked back to his desk. He sat down and put his elbows on the desk, his fingers making a steeple in front of his face.

He shook his head and sighed.

"Now, I've seen it all."

He straightened up before continuing, his frown still in place, a sign he was concentrating on what to do next.

"Anna, can you get Roberto in here as soon as he comes in?

Thank God not too many people are in yet. I'm well aware of what it might have looked like. You'll talk to Marco?

Anna nodded again.

"Yes, I've asked Marco to wait in my office, and I've already sent a message to Roberto to come straight here instead of going to Human Resources. He's on his way. Luca?"

Luca looked up.

"Yes?"

"Do you need anything? Shall I call anyone for you? I imagine that was quite a shock. And so early in the morning."

Luca frowned. He didn't want Anna to know the depth of his feelings. As the soon-to-be-new CEO of Armati, he understood only too well the necessity to remain calm and professional at all times. But Anna's use of the word shock, fell woefully short of how he'd describe his feelings. Try mad as hell, played for a fool and nauseated, and she'd be closer.

Instead, he took a deep breath and turned towards his secretary.

"Thank you for your concern, Anna. Yes, it was quite a shock. But I'll be okay."

As she turned to leave, he added.

"When you've finished talking with Marco, can you ask him or one of his waiters to remove my breakfast things? I'm not hungry, and I'll need the table for my meetings later. But I'd like some coffee, please."

Anna nodded and left, closing the door behind her.

Luca leaned back in his chair and put his arms behind his head.

Fia had been clever. He had to give her that. She worked hard and everyone sang her praises, including the head of department for whom she'd worked before. Her record was spotless, and all who worked with her, considered her a mover and shaker. Otherwise, Luca would never have contemplated hiring her as his secretary. She seemed perfectly positioned for the promotion.

Memories of her interview flitted across Luca's mind. She'd presented very different on that day, spoke with intelligence and had clearly come to the interview, not only well prepared, but expecting to get the position. She was charming and warm, and just the right amount of professional distance had convinced him she was the right person to replace Santina, although in reality, no one ever could. It hadn't occurred to him Enzo would want to retire so soon and that Anna, who he'd always known he'd inherit at some point, would be available to him. Damn, why hadn't Enzo just talked to him. If Luca had known of Enzo's plans then, he would never even have interviewed or hired anyone else.

Luca ran his fingers through his hair and rested his head in his hands.

Where had he gone wrong? Usually a good judge of character, how had he not seen Fia for the little viper she was?

God, what a start to the day.

He sighed.

That wasn't true. It had started just great. But Fia evidently had the idea to spoil things. What was she thinking? He'd never given her any sign he was interested in her as a woman.

Suddenly, Luca's heart skipped a beat as his thoughts turned to the past.

Shit! Well, there was that one time... But it was so long ago, it was only the once and he'd been extremely drunk. He remembered waking up afterwards and going in search of water to quench his alcohol-induced thirst. He'd been appalled at the state of him and his actions had swarmed into his brain like a tsunami. It had sobered him up fast.

How idiotic was he to favor one of the young women who worked at Armati? He'd always in the past chosen a model to share his bed for the night, or sometimes a little longer. But there had been something about Fia that night. Maybe he was drunker than usual. It had meant nothing.

Obviously, Fia had harbored a difference of opinion all this time. But how had he not noticed it? He'd been so focused on Naomi. Santina had to point out to him that something was going on with Fia.

He could kick himself for his stupidity. In the not-too-distant past, he would've seen it for himself. The only conclusion he could come to, not that it was an excuse by any means, was Naomi had blinded him in the best way possible. Her purity had made him forget the deviousness of women like Fia.

Luca was still thinking along those lines when a knock on his door told him Roberto had arrived.

Friends since pre-school, Roberto immediately believed Luca without question when Luca told him what had happened. Still, everything would need to be done by the law of the land so there would be no repercussions later on.

Director of Armati's Human Resources, Roberto could use his law degree to deal with the two young women.

Luca knew he could trust his old friend.

CHAPTER 7

*E*ven though the morning's events had kept their foothold in his mind, Luca's day had turned out far more hectic than he could have expected. Meetings could not be moved and followed one after another.

He'd had to forego lunch, grabbing a few handfuls of nuts here and there and keeping his energy levels topped up by drinking copious amounts of coffee. He'd pay for it later, no doubt, when sleep would become an unattainable caffeine induced hallucination. His stomach grumbled from hunger and the harsh mistreatment during the day.

He had half an hour before catching up with Roberto in his final meeting of the day. Luca was just about to order some food when his phone buzzed in his pocket. When he looked down at it in his hand, he noticed simultaneously the call was from Naomi and it was already far later than he'd realized.

Where did the day go?

He'd intended to call Naomi much earlier, but things just kept getting in the way, somehow. How the hell did he allow the day to pass by without getting in touch with Naomi? He'd have to work harder at breaking his bachelor habits now he was married and had a wife to consider, particularly where work was concerned.

The moment he heard her high-toned, tight tear-stained voice, he knew his day at the office was over.

"Luca? Are you still at the office?"

Quickly, he gathered his things together, grabbed his keys and waved to Anna as he ran from his office. In his other hand, he held the phone clamped to his ear. He tried to keep his voice level as he sprinted to his car, opened the door and threw things onto the passenger's seat. As he started the engine, the blue tooth connection with his phone came on in the car. He threw his phone on the passenger seat and kept talking to Naomi on the car's built-in system as the powerful sports engine roared. Luca raced out of the parking lot and down the road.

While he was talking to Naomi and doing his best to sound calm, his mind was speeding faster than the car. He couldn't get much information out of her other than that she was deeply upset.

Who the hell had phoned her?

It had to have been another of Fia's cronies because she and her photographer friend were still at the police station as far as he knew. If he found out Fia had somehow instructed someone else to call Naomi to fill her in on some fabricated version of what had happened in his office, heads would roll.

Luca's car skidded to a halt in front of their villa. He ran to the front door, leaving his car door open in his haste to get to Naomi.

She was everything to him. He wouldn't let anything come between them, especially not a delusional fantasy concocted by some devious little bitch like Fia.

He had to swallow the fury he felt towards the girl fast so he could be there for Naomi.

Luca was grateful the front door was unlocked because he didn't think his fingers could work the key to get it open. He was shaking from head to toe as he threw open the door and ran inside.

Naomi was sitting on the marble staircase. Her knees were drawn up to her chest, her arms hugging her legs closer to her. Blonde hair spilled over her legs and arms.

Luca bolted up the stairs, sank down beside her and tried to take her into his arms.

She wouldn't let him. Her body was stiff, and she wrapped her arms tighter around her knees.

He lifted her hair away from her face.

"Naomi, amore mio? Please, tell me what happened. Don't shut me out. We can deal with this. Please?"

As she turned her face away from him, he saw from the puffy redness around her eyes, she'd been crying for some time.

He tried again.

"Amore? Please? I know I should've called you this morning to tell you what had happened with Fia. But things got so hectic and crazy at work I just didn't get a chance. I'm so sorry. Please, at least hear my side?"

Naomi turned towards him so quickly he had to back away a little to make sure they didn't both go tumbling down the staircase.

Her eyes narrowed and her nostrils flared.

"What! You mean there's more? That something else happened today? Why wouldn't you tell me about these things? Why did I have to receive video evidence of your sordid past with Fia? But it's not in the past is it? It's still ongoing. Is that why you hired her as your secretary? So you two could continue your sexual games? I trusted you, Luca. I gave myself to you and I thought you were mine. But now...!"

Naomi jumped up and ran to the bedroom and into her dressing room. She grabbed a bag and started indiscriminately piling clothes into it.

Behind her, Luca who had followed her, watched in paralysed astonishment.

"Wait! What are you doing? Where are you going?"

Luca tried to stop Naomi by grabbing her arm, but she shrugged him off.

She continued throwing things in the bag and spoke without looking at him.

"Away from you and your Fia. No wonder you invited her to sit with us at Enzo's party. And to think I endured her bitchiness because I didn't want to upset your working relationship with her... I'm so disappointed in you, Luca. I don't want to see you right now...after all we've been through, after all you've said to me... To find out you're sleeping with your secretary under my nose and we've only been married a few months. Well, all I can say is I'm glad I found it out now and not later, when you would've ruined my life completely."

Naomi was crying again, but she did her best to hide it from him. She kept her back to him and stopped talking when the tears threatened to change her voice.

Luca couldn't believe what was happening. First, Fia dropped a bombshell on him this morning, and now the love of his life was packing a bag, convinced he was having an affair with Fia? What the hell was going on?

He was pretty sure Fia hadn't had the opportunity today to contact Naomi. Instead, he should've done so. But now wasn't the time to beat himself up about his inadequacies.

He had to find out what the bloody hell Naomi was talking about.

"Please amore, please tell me what happened. I promise on my heart I'm one hundred percent not having an affair with Fia, nor have I ever had one. Please..."

Naomi wiped her eyes on her hand and swung around to face her husband.

"How can you say that when I have evidence!"

It was Luca's turn to narrow his eyes.

"What do you mean you have evidence? What evidence?"

Naomi thrust her phone at him.

"This. And don't try to deny it. It's all there."

Luca took the phone and watched in horror a video taken on the night of that fateful party he barely remembered. It focused on an extremely drunk Luca chasing Fia, amidst a very busy party. People were milling around, dancing, drinking, laughing and having a great time. But the video honed in on a giggling Luca and Fia as they tumbled into the hot tub ignoring the other people already in there. They got down to some serious kissing and undressing. Then, a clearly aroused Luca took Fia's hand and pulled her upstairs to his bedroom where they had vigorous and explicitly uninhibited sex.

Luca could feel himself sweating. Watching the video was like watching a stranger who looked and sounded exactly like him. He didn't even recognize himself in those actions. Who the hell had filmed the video?

The fury he'd suppressed earlier, bubbled to the surface making his voice sound hard.

"Where did you get this?"

Naomi lifted her chin in defiance to the threat she heard in his voice even though she knew his anger wasn't aimed at her.

"How do I know who it's from? It must be someone who has access to our personal information. How else could they have found my number?"

Naomi was right. God, he'd have to have a thorough investigation of the people working at Armati. What a fiasco, just at his busiest time when things were about to take off on several projects simultaneously. He really didn't need this right now.

He ran a hand through his hair. Roberto would know what to do.

Luca looked for his phone to call Roberto and then remembered that it was still outside in his car. But before he could get hold of Roberto to deal with the personnel issue, he had to make things right with Naomi, first.

"Amore, about this video..."

Luca spoke quickly, afraid she wouldn't hear him out and walk out of his life for good if he couldn't convince her he was speaking the truth. He explained how uncharacteristic it was what had happened that night, and how having seen the video for himself, he could hardly believe his actions. He explained he hadn't known of the video's existence until now and couldn't imagine who had taken it and why. Many people had taken videos that night. It was a normal thing to do at parties. It had never occurred to him one of those videos would not only be focussed on his actions, but it would be used in this way.

Naomi stood still as a desert rock. Only her eyes displayed her turbulent emotions.

Luca almost wished she was more Italian, more fiery, that she'd fight with him. Her stillness unnerved him, and he realized they'd never actually had a proper quarrel until now. No wonder he didn't know what to expect from her. She probably didn't know what to expect from him, either. But no matter their differences in this area, he was damned if he was going to let Fia be the subject of their first real argument, or their last, come to think of it. No, his main concern now was to let Naomi see the truth so they could fight Fia together.

Ironically, the video had proved the Luca he'd been then was a million miles removed from the Luca he was now.

Quickly, he told Naomi everything that had happened that morning. He left nothing out. There could be no comeback on his explanation, nothing that would be unclear or could lead to any misunderstandings.

His voice was gentle as he spoke.

"Fia had obviously been planning it for a while, and she had accomplices. She and her friend are still at the police station as far as I know. You can check everything with Anna and Marco. They were there. They saw it all."

Luca felt stupid bringing Anna and Marco's names into this. It sounded like a playground thing. But he'd do whatever it took to make Naomi understand she could believe him, that he loved her more than anything in the world and that nothing had changed as far as he was concerned.

Naomi had at least been looking at him, even though her green eyes were still cold and hurt but flashed now and then with anger as the story unfolded.

A long silence followed his words. But just when Luca thought she wouldn't say anything and wondered what else he could do, Naomi cleared her throat.

"I never imagined marrying you would bring such things, such a drama into my life, Luca. It isn't what I want -"

"Believe me, it isn't what I want, either, amore mio. All I want is you, us, our life together. I'll do anything to have that. You are the love of my soul. I don't want a life without you in it. I can't apologize enough for not calling you straight away after the episode with Fia at the office. Please believe me when I say I will regret it for the rest of my life. My only excuse is Santina was right about me being a workaholic. If ever I needed it confirmed, today did that. I'll never, ever let it happen again, I promise, amore mio."

Naomi blinked a few times. She was clearly having difficulties holding back the tears. But Luca saw in her eyes these were no longer tears of sadness and hurt. He saw when her thoughts changed, when she understood, believed him, forgave him. He saw when she realized he wasn't the man who looked and sounded like him on the video.

Luca moved towards her and held out his hand for her to take.

"Come, amore. Let's go sit somewhere more comfortable. Please?"

Naomi still wouldn't let him touch her. She walked through the bedroom, down the corridor and the stairs, and went to sit in a chair in the lounge, making it clear she didn't want him too near her.

Luca sighed and sat down on the sofa closest to her.

Why, oh why hadn't he just blown out a meeting and called her this morning? He couldn't bear that she'd turned into this cold stranger. But could he blame her? What if their roles had been reversed? How would he feel?

"I promise you again, amore, I'll never let work get in the way of us. Please can you forgive me? I genuinely intended to call you straight away this morning, but things got crazy busy. It was on my mind all day to tell you. Yes, work is important to me. You know that and I can't deny it. But today taught me the biggest lesson of my life so far. You are the most important thing in my life. Without you, none of it would matter."

Naomi sighed.

Luca could see she believed him. She must've encountered such indescribably busy days at Desert Lodge herself. He tucked her hair behind her ear and left his hand on her face for a moment, before taking her hand in his. He couldn't go on without her. Surely, she knew that by now.

"I'm so sorry you got hurt because of my actions long ago, my Naomi. You know we're cast in the strongest material, amore. None of this could ever affect us at all. I'll never leave you."

At his words, Naomi leaned towards him, and Luca felt relief that he'd guessed her worst fear correctly. So, that was what the tears earlier had been all about. He knew of her traumatic childhood when both her parents had died in a car crash, and he understood her fear that the people she loved most would leave her. But even though it had caused her pain, Luca couldn't control the warming of his heart at the confirmation he was that important to her.

He squeezed her hand to impart the importance of what he was about to say.

"I'd do anything to shield you from this or anything else that could harm you. You know that, right?"

But he hadn't, had he? First, there was crazed Stefan in Namibia and now this situation with Fia. Both had had a problem with him but took it out on Naomi. He didn't care about himself, but Naomi didn't deserve this. These people knew his weakness. If they could get to her, they could twist the knife in him. Thankfully, because of the elephants trampling Stefan to death, he was no longer a problem in their lives.

Luca's eyes narrowed as he thought about how to stop Fia from spoiling their happiness. He was sure she was behind the video on Naomi's phone. He'd need Roberto's help, and he'd make sure she'd disappear from their lives altogether.

Hours later, when they'd talked things through, and Luca had answered all Naomi's questions to her satisfaction, they remained sitting together on the sofa. Luca had dragged Naomi onto his lap, their heads resting against each other's as the setting sun slowly faded through the tall windows.

CHAPTER 8

*N*aomi had set the alarm but woke up before it was due to go off. On the pillow beside hers, Luca's beautiful face was turned towards her, finally peaceful in sleep.

It had been a trying few days. Naomi had wanted to spend as much time with Johan and Kerri, but arranging their Italian blessing had made it in into a juggling act. And the Fia fiasco, especially that video, couldn't have come at a worse time. But in her heart, Naomi had known from the first that Luca was innocent, and the video had been sent to cause problems between them deliberately.

But to see him having sex with Fia in this house, in a room she'd come to know, seemed like such a betrayal even though it had happened before she even knew of Luca's existence. Watching the scenes unfold had choked her breath in her throat and clamped her heart in an iron fist until pent-up tears ripped through the aching pain in her chest.

That Luca had rushed home to protest his innocence had convinced her finally, and she'd believed him completely.

Hadn't she experienced Fia for herself?

Naomi could well believe Fia had planned everything that happened at the party that night. How Fia imagined she'd ever get away with it was beyond Naomi. It wouldn't surprise her if Fia had spiked Luca's drink that night, either. His behavior seemed so out of character for the man she'd come to know.

Luca's shock had been clear when he'd watched the video, which further reinforced his innocence. Even if he were wilder in his younger, single days, no one changed that much, did they?

Naomi couldn't help thinking how unfair it was that something so awful had happened to Luca. He was the most kind, generous and genuine man she'd ever met. He deserved none of it. She wished there was a way she could protect him from gold digging, scheming women like Fia.

Only now did Naomi fully understand Luca's reaction when he'd overheard her conversation with Kerri at Desert Lodge that time. It must've sounded as though she, too, had been thinking of him in terms of the money and prestige he offered. Now, she understood how hearing it would have filled him with revulsion. How could it not when there were women like Fia in his life?

Thank goodness they'd worked things out between them because Naomi couldn't imagine her life without him in it. They fitted like the pieces of a puzzle, the perfection of their picture emerging only once they'd joined. On their own, they were only half the picture they'd yearned to be. This episode with Fia had just strengthened them.

But her lovely Namibian visitors and the Fia debacle was all she had to deal with. Well, that, and she was now the owner of Desert Lodge and all it entailed.

Luca, however, had many Armati projects going on simultaneously and was taking on more responsibilities now Enzo was nearing retirement.

Naomi couldn't help wondering if Luca was finding it difficult getting used to a home life with his new wife and her friends, on top of everything else. She knew if he were still single, he would've moved into his office by now, and worked all the hours God sent.

On the one hand, Naomi wanted to make things as easy as possible for Luca, but on the other, how could she not focus on what had happened? How could anyone be that vindictive, or crazy, or whatever was wrong with Fia?

Naomi had to admit that Johan and Kerri's visit was a welcome distraction. It was difficult to believe they'd already been here for an entire week. Naomi loved having them around and showing them her Italy and her new life.

Kerri being the sister Naomi had never had, was a joy both women relished. So, it was thrilling to have Kerri here and share in her happiness with Johan. How much better would it have been were Naomi able to focus only on their visit and fully enjoy them while they were here?

In her unguarded moments, however, there Fia would be. It made Naomi resent Fia more even as she tried her best to banish the girl from lurking at the back of her mind.

Naomi yawned and stretched and thought she could detect the aroma of coffee. It was quite possible Signora Giana had already arrived despite the early hour.

Slowly, Naomi got out of bed. Let Luca have a lie-in. Her poor husband had been through the wars lately and deserved his rest. She tip-toed to her bathroom, even though she was sure her steps would be silent on their plush bedroom carpet.

From her bathroom, she had easy access to her walk-in wardrobe, and quickly got dressed, scrunching her hair into a loose ponytail. Jeans and a t-shirt would be perfectly comfortable for a day of preparations. No doubt, it would include last-minute running about for tonight's celebrations.

Thoughts about the event turned Naomi's focus to Anna. The woman had been a godsend. Anna had been Enzo's assistant for years. No wonder Enzo sang her praises and Luca wanted her to work for him when Enzo retired. Anna had coordinated everything with the top wedding planner in the area. Everything had run smoothly so far, and Naomi had little to contribute, other than her home. It was such a relief, especially given the problems with Fia. There were no doubting Anna's secretarial and organizational skills, but more importantly, she was a million miles away from everything Fia represented.

The villa seemed quiet enough, though Naomi fancied she could sense the others' presence. It felt comforting, and once again, Naomi basked in the feeling of being home, of belonging, of having found her place.

As she neared the bottom of the stairs, she could make out the familiar sounds of Signora Giana in the kitchen.

The older lady gave a little start, her hand going to her ample bosom when Naomi appeared suddenly in the doorway. But soon, Signora Giana was smiling again and poured Naomi a mug of freshly brewed Italian coffee. With her other hand, Signora Giana put a finger on her lips and with eyes widened, produced an exaggerated "shhh," a sign they should be quiet, as though Naomi didn't already know that.

Naomi couldn't help smiling at the melodrama she'd come to expect from Signora Giana. It reminded her of another of the Signora's traits she admired.

When Naomi had told her about the stories she'd been writing down, the older woman encouraged Naomi to have them published. But only after she'd seen them first, of course, to add details or correct something Naomi got wrong, or to embellish further on the already scandalous goings-on.

Naomi had decided the proceeds, should there be any, should go to Signora Giana. At first, Signora Giana was dead against it and agreed with Luca when he'd wondered why Naomi would give away money she'd earned. But Naomi had argued she didn't exactly need the money, and if the book made any money at all, it could be a good little pension for Signora Giana. When Naomi explained it was the only way she'd feel comfortable publishing the stories, both Signora Giana and Luca had finally conceded.

Naomi was still having coffee when several delivery men arrived bearing boxes of produce to be turned into a fabulous dinner for Johan and Kerri's blessing that evening. Signora Giana instantly became the Sargent Major of the kitchen. She appeared to take enormous pleasure in ordering the men about and making sure they put the boxes well out of her way.

Naomi had to bite her lip more than once to stop from laughing out loud at the older woman's antics and the men's growing exasperation at her demands and bossiness.

When it all became too much for Naomi, she left them to it.

Outside the kitchen door, she stood for moments on the steps to admire the view over the back garden. The early morning in this region of Italy was a particularly glorious experience. But the air had a pleasant bite to it despite the beautiful blue sky and happy sunlight dancing through the trees.

Naomi ran her hand over her arm over sudden goosebumps appearing at the early sign that the year was soon coming to an end.

She walked past the cars and vans parked on the gravel near the kitchen door, through the herb garden and the trees, and along the side of the building to the front of the villa where a marquee had already been erected for the evening's event. She knew that Johan and Kerri thought Luca's insistence on giving them a proper party was sweet. Luca had invited several staff members from Armati to the celebration. Kerri's beaming smiles at the news showed she was especially excited about meeting them as she'd got to know them online when they'd been working together on the dune buggies for Desert Lodge. Naomi knew Kerri felt she'd be meeting old friends for the first time.

Naomi walked through the marquee where tables and chairs had already been arranged. Bottles of wine from the Armati vineyards and rows of delicate glasses populated the bar area along the side. Everything looked as though it was coming along just fine and there was nothing for her do but admire others' work. As Naomi continued to walk among the tables, she thought it would be a great idea that the four of them go out for breakfast, perhaps to Osteria Francescana, famous for its fabulous breakfasts. It would get them out from under the feet of the people working to get everything ready. Perhaps Enzo, Santina and Roberto could join them there?

She took her phone out of her pocket to check the time. But the moment she touched it, it rang. It wasn't a number she recognized. Just about to reject the call, she changed her mind thinking it might be someone to do with the celebrations. As she'd wanted to help as much as she could, she had allowed Anna to pass on her details to the wedding planner and a few of her staff.

"Hello?"

No reply.

"Hello? Can I help you?"

Again, no answer and then the line went dead.

Whoever it was probably realized it was a wrong number when Naomi answered in English, or it may have been one of the staff members who were unconfident speaking English. They'd most likely find Anna, instead.

Naomi checked the time and replaced the phone in her pocket. She wondered if the others were awake yet? It had only just gone eight o'clock. It was a miracle she was awake that early herself.

But her mind wouldn't shut up about Fia. That, together with the excitement of getting ready for her friends' blessing, and that she'd be returning to Desert Lodge soon, was probably to blame for her uncharacteristic sleep patterns lately.

Her coffee finished, and satisfied that everything was going to plan, Naomi left the marquee.

As she was about to walk back the way she'd come, she saw a red Fiat 500 driving up the driveway. It was the car of choice for many young Italian professionals. But Anna had given clear instructions no one was to use the driveway at the front of the house today. It was reserved for friends and guests only. Otherwise, it could cause an almighty traffic jam. The delivery men all used the other driveway that took them directly to the kitchen. Like Anna, Luca and the rest, even Naomi had been using the other driveway.

Naomi squinted against the sun. She didn't recognize the car, and she couldn't make out the driver at this distance. Perhaps it was one of Luca's friends? But this early? Could it be he'd asked someone to come over for an early morning meeting? If he had, he'd forgotten to tell her.

As the car drew closer, Naomi could make out a woman's long hair. The car stopped under the last big trees before the driveway opened around the circular patch of lawn in front of the villa. But before the door opened, Naomi had a sudden sense of doom. She knew without a shadow of a doubt the young woman who came walking towards her, was Fia.

Fia stopped a few feet away from Naomi, her hands on her hips.

Naomi stayed where she was and raised her voice just a little. She wanted Fia to hear her properly.

"What are you doing here, Fia?"

Fia shook her hair, her chin pointing defiantly upwards, before answering.

"Now I've lost my job at Armati, I thought I'd make myself useful with the celebrations you're having this evening. You know...now I'm unemployed because of you."

"I won't argue with you, Fia. But you brought your current situation on yourself. It had nothing to do with me."

Naomi thought she must've imagined it, but it looked as though Fia had stomped her foot.

Fia's face flushed red, and her voice took on a brittle high-pitched sound.

"It had everything to do with you. Luca was practically mine. Until you showed up. All this...!"

She waved her arms about, her voice rising ever higher.

"...was practically mine. Luca probably never told you about our night together here, did he? How he chose me. He invited me into his hot tub, into his bed. Probably the same bed you now share with him. But he chose me, first. Do you hear me? He chose me."

Fia had been walking closer and closer towards Naomi with each withering sentence. Only now, did Naomi notice how disheveled Fia was. Her makeup was smudged and cracked as though she'd slept in it. Her hair was unbrushed and greasy. Her top bore stains down the front, and her skirt was twisted. Her bare legs looked out of place with her smart office shoes that bore scuff marks Naomi was sure wasn't part of Fia's usual style.

Naomi was still wondering if she should feel sorry for Fia when she launched herself at Naomi. Fia screamed her fury as she ran at Naomi, her hands stretched out in front of her, her fingers claw-like.

Naomi looked around for something to defend herself with or for someone to help stop the frenzied girl. But everyone must have still been around the back or in the kitchen. She faced Fia but felt numb as the shock sunk in of seeing the girl transform from a normal looking human being into a screaming, yelling creature she didn't recognize.

What the hell? Was Fia mentally unstable?

Naomi knew she had to move, do something, but the unexpectedness of Fia's outburst had frozen her in place. Her heart was beating wildly, and she was aware her breathing had increased, but her mouth was entirely dry, her voice locked up. Everything seemed to be happening in slow motion.

Feeling detached and as though watching the scene through water, Naomi saw Fia getting closer and closer. The hysterical girl didn't seem to need to breathe as she was still screaming at the top of her lungs without a pause. Naomi couldn't understand a single word but instinctively stepped aside as Fia ran at her. Fia ran past her, seemingly unable to stop her momentum. Naomi turned around in time to see Fia doing the same. Fia's eyes were wild and hate-filled, her mouth was distorted, and the whiteness around her lips betrayed her out-of-control fury. Her voice went up a note or two more until the shrillness coming from her mouth became the thing that unfroze Naomi.

It was sudden, like the snapping of a finger, to bring Naomi back to herself and the reality of Fia facing her. But the sound coming from Fia was like nothing Naomi had ever heard before, and it was difficult to resist the urge to cover her ears. She knew Fia was using words, but all Naomi could hear was the high-pitched screeching sounds that carried no meaning.

Behind Fia, the villa's front door suddenly flew open. Kerri, Johan and Luca ran out simultaneously. Evidently, everyone had still been in bed as all were in their pajamas. Johan grabbed Fia's right arm and Luca her left. Between them, they barely restrained her as she stomped on their bare feet with her heels and tried to bite their fingers on her arms.

Following them, Signora Giana appeared hands on her hips, a disapproving scowl on her face, and Anna at her side with her phone in her hand.

Another car screeched to a halt near them, spraying gravel in all directions. Roberto and a guard jumped out. As Luca and Johan fought to keep Fia from trying to attack them or anyone else, Roberto apologized breathlessly.

Apparently, Fia had somehow slipped away from the security guard he'd arranged to watch her home. When the guard called him to report her missing, Roberto drove to their villa at once where he'd suspected she might be heading.

His face was ashen as he addressed Luca. His rapid speech and the sweat on his brow showed his annoyance and disbelief that Fia was already here causing havoc.

Naomi only half-listened to Roberto because Signora Giana had marched down the steps and was standing mere inches away from Fia, her finger wagging dangerously close to Fia's nose.

Signore Giana's musical voice projected through the morning air, as she spoke in English with her heavy Italian accent, clearly for Johan's and Kerri's benefit.

"I know your papa, you silly girl. How he will feel shame you behaving like this."

She waved her arms about to include everyone.

"You shame everybody. And our visitors."

Signora Giana's words had a miraculous effect on Fia who stopped struggling at once. Fia practically collapsed in Luca's arms, crying and begging his forgiveness.

Naomi wasn't convinced it wasn't yet another Fia act. She wanted to pull the girl off her husband but restrained herself. There was no way she'd want to come across as demented as Fia did. It was difficult to do, but Naomi focused on Signore Giana, instead, proud that the English lessons she'd given the older woman were paying off.

Apparently, Luca wasn't falling for Fia's wiles, either. He shoved Fia towards the guard, who'd been staring at Fia. The guard's face was white with shock and his eyes wide in disbelief. But hearing Luca's voice, he came suddenly to life and cuffed Fia, holding on to her tightly. It was clear he had no intention of allowing her to escape from him, again.

Luca took long strides to stand beside Naomi, putting a protective arm around her shoulders.

"Are you okay, amore mio?"

Naomi nodded and leaned into Luca, relief flooding her body it was all over.

She noticed Anna had also walked down the stairs, her phone still in her hand. But instead, of staying with the group, Anna was walking away from them, down the road towards the sound of police sirens that screamed in the distance and announced their imminent arrival by their flashing blue lights.

CHAPTER 9

*B*y the time Santina arrived to see she could contribute anything to Johan and Kerri's celebration, things had settled down again into ordered chaos. Fia's dramas were temporarily forgotten.

But when Santina heard what had happened, she was outraged. She fussed like a mother elephant over her ellies, checking and re-checking that Luca and Naomi were okay. Naomi thought it was endearing. Luca not so much.

The villa and the marquee in front of it had become a hive of activity, meanwhile. Flowers and extra plants had been delivered, and the wedding planner's staff were busy arranging everything. Waiters and waitresses were polishing glasses and cutlery and setting the tables in the marquee. Boxes of wine and champagne had been delivered and stowed in the cellar below the kitchen.

In the kitchen, Signora Giana was busy perfecting finger food masterpieces for the luncheon drinks party. Marco and several staff members had arrived to prep for the evening's dinner. Signora Giana had reluctantly, and with several exasperated sighs, divided the kitchen in half. She was using the left side, and Marco had taken possession of the right side. Thankfully, they could stay out of each other's way as the villa's enormous kitchen accommodated both comfortably. Their worlds only collided at the double sinks beneath the large windows where Signora Giana made a big show of allowing her guests priority while making sure they never forget whose kitchen it was.

Santina tactfully suggested that she drive Luca and Johan to the restaurant where Enzo and Roberto were waiting for them. It gave Naomi and Kerri time to catch up as they quickly went through the outfits for Kerri to wear on her special day. For now, she followed Naomi and Santina's example and donned jeans and a t-shirt for breakfast.

Naomi grabbed her keys and handbag and led the way downstairs. Kerri followed her friend through the front door and slid into the car beside Naomi.

"I'm glad breakfast is informal. I was worried that I'd have to be dressed up all the time. The Italian ladies always seem so put together, don't you think?"

Naomi smiled.

"I know what you mean. It seems that way. But I don't think it's true. Santina's style, although still sophisticated, can be very relaxed. And I've remained informal, as you can see. I don't think I'll change in that regard soon."

Kerri glanced at her friend.

"You've always been stylish, so I'm not surprised you fit in here perfectly. You could wear a bin bag and still look amazing."

"Oh, what a lovely thing to say. I think you could wear a bin bag and look a million dollars, too, so touché."

Naomi smiled at her friend.

"Seriously, though, I'm so glad I get to spend your special day with you. Especially, here, where I feel like I've come home to myself."

Kerri touched Naomi's arm to emphasize her words.

"So am I, hun. And I know what you mean. Isn't it interesting how everyone has their place in the world? It isn't always where you were born or where your family lives. I can see this is your place. You seem to have grown more into yourself here. I'm so happy for you. But how do you feel about returning to Desert Lodge again, soon?"

As though she was choosing her words carefully, Naomi took a moment to reply.

"I know it's only been months, but it feels as though I've been away for far longer. I'm looking forward to seeing everything you've put in place, and I'm excited to see everyone. Most of all, I can't wait to smell the desert, again. But I'm a little worried about Luca. He's in the middle of several major projects. I don't know how easy he'll find it to leave here."

Kerri frowned.

"I know you guys said six months here and six months there. But do you think Luca's changed his mind and wants to make it shorter in Namibia?"

Naomi glanced at her friend before turning her eyes back on the road. Relief flooded her that Kerri had broached it. Even though she hadn't discussed it with Luca yet, she'd always known he might find the six-month gap away from Italy hard. Now, with as many projects as he had on the go, she didn't want him to feel torn between her and his beloved Armati.

"Would you mind if it was shorter? You don't need me there for longer, do you?"

"No, I guess it'll be fine. But I'll miss you. Skyping isn't the same, is it?"

Kerri was silent for a moment, her thoughts reflected in her expressive eyes.

"Can I say something about the Fia situation?"

"Of course. Shoot."

Kerri sighed as though she was preparing herself for Naomi's negative reaction to what she was about to say.

"Was it just me or do you think something is going on between Fia and the guard?"

Naomi glanced at her friend.

"You mean the one Robert brought along this morning?"

"Yes. Something about him seemed off."

"In what way?"

"I don't know...the way he looked at Fia... I got the feeling they're involved, somehow."

Naomi thought about it for a moment.

"But Fia has made it clear she wants Luca. Isn't it what her harassment and bizarre behavior have been all about?"

"Maybe. Maybe not. Maybe blackmail is ultimately her aim."

Naomi pursed her lips before responding.

"Well, she's not subtle about it, is she?"

Kerri flapped a hand in the air, as though she was swatting away a fly.

"Don't mind me. I don't want to add to your worries. It's probably just my overactive imagination."

But Kerri's words had created a new level of anxiety in Naomi's mind. She knew Kerri had more experience with men than she did, and Kerri was a keen observer of people. Naomi had always respected that ability in Kerri. But Naomi didn't want to believe there could be yet another element to the already messy situation.

Naomi forced the negative thoughts from her mind and concentrated on her driving, instead. She put the car into a lower gear as they neared the restaurant and looked for parking. Luckily, someone pulled out of a space just as they arrived, and she parked the car in front of the restaurant.

The others were sitting at a table near the large windows that gave onto the bustling road in front of the restaurant. When Enzo saw Naomi and Kerri getting out of the Armati, he came to the door to greet them before leading them to the table. Enzo waited until they'd greeted everyone and were comfortably seated before proposing a toast.

He raised his glass of orange juice laced with prosecco and smiled at Kerri and Johan.

"To our wonderful friends from Africa."

Everyone clinked glasses, and amid much laughter and excited talk, Naomi's heart felt as though it was bursting with gratitude her life had turned out so brilliantly and she got to share it with these people whom she loved like family. She looked at the dear faces around the table. They may not be related by blood, but they'd chosen each other, and surely that was as valid as blood family, wasn't it?

When she focussed on the conversation again, she realized Roberto was talking about Fia.

He turned to her.

"I'm sorry you had to see that video, Naomi. But Luca has told me you're not in favor of him pressing charges. And unless he does..."

Roberto shrugged and spread his hands. He didn't need to spell it out there was nothing more he could do about the situation with Fia.

Naomi nodded and folded her arms.

She hadn't made up her mind about Fia, but realized her input could have serious repercussions. Did she want it on her conscience that her contribution could be the downfall of another human being, no matter what Fia did?

Who knows what was going on for Fia, anyway? Maybe she had a mental illness? But shouldn't Fia be judged in a court of law? It might even help her.

Things just didn't add up in Naomi's mind, and Kerri's words in the car helped to magnify her confusion.

It couldn't harm voicing her thoughts to Roberto, though, could it?

"I still think she probably spiked Luca's drink. You saw the video?"

Before Roberto could respond, Luca, who was sitting on her other side, leaned towards her.

His face was serious and his dark eyes intense when he spoke.

"You never told me that, amore. What made you think it?"

Naomi knew Luca had been shocked and puzzled when he'd seen the video. But she also knew Luca had full faith in Robert, whom he had assured her, would investigate everything thoroughly. The truth would be revealed, Luca had claimed rather dramatically. But she knew it was just his way of bringing lightness to the situation. All they had to do was wait, albeit impatiently. Like Luca, Naomi had prayed the Fia fiasco would disappear as quickly as possible.

Naomi put her hand on Luca's forearm.

"You saw the video, my love. It didn't look like your behavior at all. And you said you couldn't remember any of it afterwards. I don't know... It's just a thought. But you hear about people's drinks being spiked all the time, don't you? Seeing you like that... The Luca on the video was completely inconsistent with who I've known you to be from the moment I'd met you."

Luca folded his arms across his chest. His tight jawline was the only sign he was listening.

Roberto leaned in from Naomi's other side.

"That's a serious allegation, Naomi. But having seen the video for myself, I feel you may have a point. Although I must confess, the more worrying aspect for me is why the video exists at all? Who took it and why did it only surface now? I feel there's more to it than we can currently see."

Roberto was silent for a moment, the frown between his eyes deepening.

"I've known Luca since we were children. You're right about him not being himself in the video, Naomi. I hadn't thought about it before, but now you mention it... There's a real possibility that Luca could have been drugged. It would be impossible to prove after all this time, of course. If true, Fia may not have drugged him herself. She seems unstable but clever, and unless she confesses to it..."

Roberto shrugged again before continuing.

"Somehow, I doubt we'll ever find out."

Naomi glanced at Luca before speaking to Roberto.

"I think there is someone else who knows what happened that night. Perhaps now she'd be in trouble because of Fia, she might talk to us? Or perhaps to the police?"

Luca took Naomi's hand.

"Amore mio, why did you never talk about this before? How could you know?"

Santina, who was sitting beside Luca, had been following the conversation.

Santina leaned forward so she could get all three in view.

"Naomi is right. I remember the afternoon before Enzo's birthday party. We went to Luigi's restaurant to check that everything was ready for the evening. Naomi went to the restroom. I remember seeing Fia and a friend following Naomi in there. When they came out, I knew something bad had happened. But only when Naomi appeared several minutes later, could I see from her face they'd said nasty things about her in there, clearly knowing she'd understand them. It was then you'd heard something about the party at Luca's villa, wasn't it, Naomi?"

Naomi nodded, astonished at Santina's perceptiveness.

"Yes. I don't know who the other girl was, but they were talking about the night of the party. It didn't make much sense then, other than to torment me. But now I've met Fia, and seen the video, I remember what they'd said. I distinctly remember Fia saying it wasn't easy to get the drug from the internet. She said it in context to the party. What else could she have meant?"

When Luca turned to look at her, Naomi noticed his face was drained and white, and his voice sounded soft from shock.

"Amore, you never told me this -"

Naomi put her arm around her husband.

"I've only just worked it out, Luca. I'm sorry. If I'd put two and two together earlier, I would have told you."

Roberto leaned back in his chair, an arm across his body, holding up his elbow on his other arm so his hand could cup his chin. A deep frown emphasized the marks between his eyes.

"Your words aren't a complete surprise to Luca or me, Naomi. We had wanted to keep our suspicions a secret, but I can see you're thinking in the same direction we did."

He winked conspiratorially at Naomi.

"I know no one wants a scandal, either for Luca personally or for Armati. And I promise to handle things with care, but especially our suspicions around the drugs, will take time to investigate."

He turned to Luca.

"My advice, my friend, is that you should go to Namibia as you'd originally planned. I know you thought of staying here longer to oversee the latest projects, but you have brilliant staff here, and Enzo hasn't retired yet."

Roberto glanced at Enzo, whose face was as grave as his son's.

Enzo nodded in agreement.

Santina put a hand on Luca's arm.

"And I will return to work with Enzo and Anna while you're gone, Luca. It will only be for the time it takes Roberto to sort out this mess Fia has created. So, you won't have a thing to worry about here."

Luca nodded and put his hand over Santina's to confirm his agreement and show his gratitude.

Roberto cleared his throat and continued.

"Things will be handled sensitively, Luca, I promise. While you're in Namibia and away from any media frenzy here, we can let the authorities deal with Fia as they see fit. Meanwhile, I'll leave no stone unturned to find out what happened that night and what this is all about. By the time you return six months later, things should've blown over enough here that you and Naomi would be left in peace."

Kerri caught Naomi's eye as she gave her friend a smile filled with relief for them both.

They'd spend the full six months together at Desert Lodge, after all.

CHAPTER 10

*N*aomi could feel the dissonance in Luca's energy. She could hardly blame him.

Not only would he not be in Italy to see through some projects he'd put into action, but there was nothing more he could do about the Fia situation. It was in Roberto's hands now to do the best he could. But ultimately, it would depend on the quality of the investigation.

Roberto's words at breakfast had been no surprise to Naomi. She'd known Luca had changed his mind about them staying in Namibia for the entire six months he'd originally proposed. But she also knew he wouldn't go against Roberto's recommendation they do so this time. Naomi couldn't help being excited at the prospect of spending the entire six months in Namibia, even though she also felt guilty for feeling it.

She was just putting on her other pearl earring and wriggling her feet into her shoes when Kerri knocked on her bedroom door.

"Wow, you look so authentically Italian, you know. I love that style of dress on you."

Naomi laughed at the expression on her friend's face.

She had chosen the light blue shift dress with care as she'd wanted Kerri to be the star of her party. Not that it was difficult for Kerri. Her amazing red curls always caught the attention no matter what she wore. Tonight, Kerri's sleeveless emerald green dress was the perfect foil for her hair.

Naomi gave her friend a hug.

"And you are completely gorgeous as always. I'm excited for you and Johan. Are you ready?"

"Well, if the great breakfast and the lovely luncheon party was anything to go by, I'm beyond excited for tonight's celebration. Signora Giana outdid herself at lunch. Marco has a lot to live up to tonight."

The friends linked arms and walked down the short corridor from the bedrooms towards the double marble staircase. But when they reached the mezzanine level just before continuing their descent down the stairs, both stopped to admire the vision before them.

Naomi gestured toward the plants and trees that had transformed the foyer into an atrium oasis for the lunch party.

"I love the way the green of the plants contrasts with the marble, don't you? I might just keep it that way and not send back any of the plants or trees. I don't know why I'd never thought of doing something like this before."

Kerri followed her friend's gesture.

"Hmm...if I stand there long enough, I'd disappear amidst your jungle in this dress."

Both women found the image hilarious, especially because both came from a country covered in sand. They held hold on to each other as they laughed until tears threatened to ruin their makeup.

They were still laughing when Luca's voice reached them.

"There you are."

Neither Naomi nor Kerri could see him as he stood camouflaged among the plants. This sent them into another fit of giggles. But their laughter faded and was replaced by gasps of wonder as the double front door opened.

The sun was just setting over the treetops, and dusk was bringing out the stars in a darkening sky. It heightened the magic of the space outside. The marquee had been decorated with fairy lights and the tall fire poles leading the way from the villa's front door to the marquee, lent an extra element of awe to the fantasy.

Kerri grabbed Naomi's arm and breathed in on an elongated "Ooh!"

When she spoke, her voice sounded sharp with excitement.

"It's the most amazing thing I've ever seen."

She turned to her friend, her green eyes bright with excitement and unshed tears of joy.

"Thank you for the best gift ever."

Naomi hugged her friend.

"You deserve the best. And I'm so delighted to be a part of your happiness. The best gift I've ever had is to share this with you."

Luca appeared at the bottom of the staircase.

"What do you mean, amore mio? The Armati I gave you isn't the best gift you've ever had? I'm deeply offended."

He placed a rather camp hand over his brow to show his disappointment, which elicited a new burst of giggles from the women. Satisfied he'd received the reaction he was after, he walked up to meet them and presented his arms so they could link with him on either side. The three of them were just about to walk down the stairs when there was a sudden bright flash outside.

At first, they thought it was yet another fabulous treat arranged by the wedding planner. But when the waiters and other staff came running towards the villa, screaming and yelling, the smiles and banter faded from the threesome.

Luca disengaged himself from his wife and her friend and dashed down the stairs. Johan, who'd been having a drink with

Enzo, Santina and their guests in the lounge, rushed out at the same time.

Luca grabbed Marco to ask what was going on, but the chef was too distressed to talk sensibly. His face was distorted and ashen as he gestured back towards the marquee. It was clear he was in shock. The first fireball had exploded right beside him. He clutched his head. A thin trickle of blood ran from his ear.

Naomi and Kerri were still frozen on the stairs. But having a higher viewpoint than the others, could see the fire, which had already eaten the back of the marquee, was blazing out of control. Long orange flames licked at the material, turning it black as the fire moved towards the front of the marquee devouring everything in its path.

The guests, the staff, Santina and Enzo stood momentarily in silence among the plants in the foyer staring at the burning marquee. It was hard to grasp.

But Roberto was at the door, his phone to his ear. Even with his back towards them, everyone could see he was extremely upset.

His voice rose above the commotion.

"You bet I'm angry! What the hell happened to the guards who were supposed to keep an eye -"

Outside, the noise from the fire trucks arriving became deafening as it sped up the road to the villa. Then, there was a swarming of firemen dowsing the burning marquee.

Anna, together with the wedding planner and several staff members stood on the steps outside, phones to their ears and urgent voices doing damage control.

Enzo approached Anna and after a quick conversation, left again. Her actions seem to go into overdrive at once. Enzo walked towards Naomi and Kerri, still standing on the marble stairs.

Naomi had an arm around Kerri, whose eyes were brimming

with tears at the realization her special Italian celebration was at an end.

Enzo touched Kerri's arm before he spoke, his voice soothing.

"We can still have your celebration, Kerri. Would you mind if we moved everything to my castle?"

Instantly, Kerri's face brightened. It was one thing Naomi had always so admired about her friend. Kerri could switch her moods so quickly and always responded positively to the slightest sign of hope in a situation.

Kerri sniffed and carefully wiped away the tears so as not to spoil her makeup. Then, she leaned towards Enzo and gave him a grateful hug.

"Oh, that would be wonderful, Enzo. How could we ever thank you?"

Enzo shrugged in that very Italian way as if to say it's no biggie.

"After you took such care of us at Desert Lodge, this is the least we can do. Come. Let's get you to the castle."

Moments later, a stylish Armati staff transporter arrived to drive the guests to the castle. Anna had already arranged for several transporters to take the staff and the food and drink to the castle. Signora Giana, the wedding planner and the waiters had gone ahead to ensure an easy transfer.

Naomi became alarmed when several trees and large plants disappeared from the foyer. But Anna reassured her she'd see them returned to the villa after the celebration.

Outside was a maelstrom of activity as the valets moved the guests' cars behind the villa safely away from the fire and the fire trucks.

The reassurance everyone felt their hard work would not go to waste, after all, produced the chaotic military precision in which things happened at speed.

By the time the guests arrived at the castle, lights had been hastily but expertly installed. It enhanced the perception of entering yet another, perhaps even better, fantasy than before. Several guests thought the fire and everything that went before, was a deliberate prelude to this production. The family said nothing to dispel the illusion. Instead, everyone breathed a collective sigh of relief.

Roberto arrived a little later. He seemed out of sorts and uncharacteristically disheveled. But after Enzo handed him a drink, patted him on the back, and Luca kissed him on both cheeks, he relaxed. His usual, affable smile returned along with what Naomi thought of as the permanent mischievous twinkle in his eye. She'd often wondered why a good-looking, lovely man like Roberto, was still single? She'd made a note to talk to Signora Giana to introduce him a suitable young lady.

Roberto took a sip of his drink before speaking.

"Fia is a slippery eel, indeed. It appears she got hold of a waiter's uniform and simply walked past the guards even though they had pictures to identify her should she turn up."

A frown had appeared on Luca's face. He interrupted Roberto.

"Well, if she'd taken that kind of initiative when she worked for me..."

Roberto contemplated his friend.

"Not only is she no longer working for you, Luca, but she's also no longer working for Armati. I've terminated her contract with us and everything else that was part of her package. She leaves with nothing, not even a pension. I wish there was more I could do to maximize her punishment. But unless we can prove she'd drugged you at the party, or she'd started the fire at the marquee, she hasn't done anything criminal."

Enzo interrupted the conversation by clapping an arm around Roberto's shoulders.

"We all know you'll do the best you can, Roberto. Come, enjoy our friends' celebration and forget about Armati matters for now."

Enzo led Roberto towards the cavernous lounge where all the other guests had congregated.

Naomi had decided from her first visit here, the reason the castle never felt cold or austere despite its size, had to be because of the many gorgeous rugs that covered the walls and floors. The furniture had been chosen with care and further lent a sense of warmth to the place.

Even though Naomi had been to the castle many times before, tonight the imposing building felt even more medieval and awesome than it usually did. The enormous chandeliers that swung gently from the high ceilings clearly helped the effect.

Naomi knew Kerri and Johan would adore every second of their time at the castle. Their celebration in Italy would be more than either could have imagined and would become a treasured memory. Naomi felt relief course through her at the thought she got to share this special night with her dearest friends and nothing, not even Fia's actions, could ruin it for them.

In an ironic twist, a fire-eater held centre stage in the lounge where his daring antics enthralled everyone. They oohed and aahed as he juggled the fiery batons high into the domed ceiling before catching them again. Then, he added more batons one after the other until they formed a fiery wheel in the air above his head. When he extinguished the last of the batons by 'eating' the fire, thunderous applause showed everyone's appreciation of his artistry.

Naomi felt herself breathe out and realized she felt relieved none of the fiery batons had caused another fire. She didn't think she could cope with any more drama that evening.

CHAPTER 11

"*H*ave you finished packing, amore mio?"

Luca was standing in the doorway to Naomi's walk-in wardrobe, one hand on his hip.

Naomi looked up from the clothes she was rolling up to maximize space in her suitcase. She'd take only a few essentials. Most of her clothes were still at Desert Lodge as Luca had insisted on buying her a whole new wardrobe in Italy. It would save her the effort of having to cart luggage from one country to another when they traveled back and forth.

She smiled at Luca and wanted to pinch herself for being so lucky. How was it he just got more handsome the more she got to know him?

"How can I finish when my gorgeous husband keeps on interrupting me?"

A slow, amused smile appeared on Luca's lips. He returned Naomi's wink.

"Flirting with me won't stop me from harassing you, Mrs Armati. You know I love you more than life itself, but we're on a deadline. Do you think we could do the packing faster?"

Naomi was still smiling as she teased her husband.

"You mean could I do the packing faster, isn't that what you meant, Mr Armati?"

Naomi winked at her husband but took on board his concerns.

"But seriously, aren't we waiting for Roberto? I thought he was coming around to update us before we leave?"

Luca sat down on Naomi's chaise longue.

"Yes, you're right, amore. Roberto will be here in..."

Luca checked his watch.

"...half an hour."

He sighed and leaned back against the curved back of the chaise longue.

Naomi watched him. He looked exhausted. Was it a good idea for him to fly them all the way to Namibia today? She wasn't so sure about it but knew there was no point raising the issue again. He'd just dismiss her fears as he had been doing since last night. That was when she'd first realized how tired he was. He'd been working hard and burning the candle at both ends, spending as much time as he could with her and their friends. That on top of the problems with Fia, had taken its toll on him. Naomi suspected he also worried about leaving Modena when all he wanted was to stay and see his projects through to the end. Perhaps going to Desert Lodge would force him to relax.

Luca ran a hand through his thick hair. When he spoke, Naomi got the impression he needed to hear the words from his mouth for it to sink into his consciousness as reality.

"I know Roberto is right. I know we have to leave. But I've never felt more unprepared. Everything will be in good hands here. My father and Santina will see to it everything happens as it should and they'll keep me informed every little step of the way, I know that..."

Naomi waited for him to continue but when he didn't, she got up from the floor where she'd been sitting next to her suitcase.

She came to sit beside Luca on the chaise and took his hand in hers.

"My Luca, I know this is hard for you. Letting go is hard. But some distance might bring even better insight, don't you think? And I don't mean about the mess Fia has created. I feel you're right to trust Roberto in that regard. I mean about your projects. They've been all-consuming, and often, when you allow yourself some distance, you can see things anew. You might come up with better ideas and solutions to the challenges you've been working on that have kept you awake lately."

Luca rubbed his thumb over the soft part between Naomi's thumb and forefinger, a small smile curling at the corners of his mouth.

"When did you become so wise, amore mio? And so psychic? How did you know I was trying to find solutions to the problems we have encountered?"

Naomi stroked the side of Luca's face with her free hand.

"My darling husband, don't you know by now I know your every expression and emotion? I can feel when things are disturbing you despite you trying to hide it from me."

Luca caught Naomi's hand in his and kissed her fingers before speaking, his dark eyes intent on hers.

"You continue to surprise and amaze me, amore mio. You're right. And you may have a point about distance perhaps bringing a fresh perspective."

He planted a soft kiss on Naomi's cheek and a longer tender kiss on her lips.

"Besides, I can't wait to spend some time alone with my gorgeous wife again."

He folded her into a warm hug, holding her as safe as she'd wanted to keep him.

Naomi allowed herself to savor for moments the lovely feeling of their bodies pressed against each other. Then, she gently nudged him away.

"I'd better finish the packing before a certain Mr Armati gets on my case again. I think he sometimes forgets I'm not a member of his adoring staff but I'm his adoring wife, instead."

Naomi got up but Luca grabbed her arm and pulled her down on his lap where he covered her face in kisses, making her squeal with laughter. Big sloppy kisses rained down on her forehead, eyelids, nose, both cheeks, chin, neck, ears and finally her lips which he captured completely.

Roberto clearing his throat from the doorway to catch their attention had the desired effect. Luca and Naomi both looked up at the sound.

Naomi could feel her face flush, but Luca continued to hold her on his lap making escape impossible. Why should she feel embarrassed to be caught kissing her husband? It was a mystery to her. Evidently, neither her husband nor Roberto thought it was anything unusual.

Roberto smiled at them as he entered the room further.

"Here you lovebirds are."

He looked around at the chaos of Naomi's packing as he spoke.

"How's the packing going?"

Naomi finally extricated herself from Luca.

She got up and went to give Roberto a hug in greeting.

"I was trying to finish the packing, but your good friend keeps on interrupting me."

Naomi smiled and winked at Luca before addressing Roberto, again.

"Can we offer you something to drink or something eat, Roberto?"

She led the way downstairs to the lounge, popping into the kitchen en route to place their orders with Signora Giana.

The older lady hadn't hidden the fact she was deeply upset about losing Luca and Naomi to Namibia for the next six months. Whenever she saw either of them, tears brimmed in her eyes. It was no different now. As Naomi was asking for tea and snacks to be served in the lounge, the Signora kept on sniffling and wiping her eyes with a handkerchief she stuffed back into the pocket of her apron.

Naomi was torn between wanting to comfort Signore Giana and joining Luca and Roberto. She didn't want to miss whatever news Roberto had brought and hoped he'd wait for her before sharing his information. She assured Signore Giana as she had done since their Namibian trip was made known to the staff, that six months would fly by.

When the older lady started to prepare their snacks, Naomi left quickly and got back to the lounge.

As Naomi entered the lounge, Luca and Roberto looked up from where they were sitting opposite each other. She went to sit on the sofa beside Luca who took her hand in his and kissed her fingers before turning his attention back to his friend.

Roberto glanced from one to the other and sat forward on the sofa, his elbows on his thighs. It looked as though he was about to share a secret.

"I know you guys are getting ready to leave for Namibia soon, so I'll try to be as brief as I can. What I'm about to tell you will come as much of a surprise to you, I'm sure, as it was to me.

"Do you remember I said that unless Fia admits to drugging you that night of the party, Luca, or admits to setting the fire that nearly destroyed your friends' wedding celebrations, there was nothing we could do?"

Luca and Naomi both nodded and waited for Roberto to continue.

"Sure, she'd been arrested for stalking you at the office that morning she'd tried her little stunt, but the police couldn't keep her. Her actions weren't criminal, and I knew we'd have a hard time proving they were. She was arrested after she'd tried to attack you, Naomi, but again, since nothing actually happened and you didn't press charges, Fia was let go once more. But the arrests over the last few days mean she's now on the police's radar. I took it upon myself to place a guard with her twenty-four-seven."

Roberto paused for a moment, the frown lines between his eyes deepening as though he was weighing his next words carefully.

His eyes found Luca's.

"I chose the guard from the security guards we employ at Armati, and you know how stringently they are vetted. We have to make sure they're completely trustworthy."

Again, Roberto paused for moments.

Naomi had the impression whatever Roberto had to say was difficult perhaps because he feared the repercussions?

When Roberto continued this time, he stared at a spot on the floor halfway between his shoes and the coffee table that separated the two sofas on which they sat.

"I chose Dino Ricci. You know him well."

Luca's eyes widened in surprise, but he waited for Roberto to continue.

Roberto nodded, his eyebrows up as if to say Luca's reaction didn't surprise him.

"Dino, as you know, is someone who'd been with Armati for many years. He'd proven his loyalty to the company and to the Armati family. I had no reason to doubt his competence or his professionalism or his loyalty."

Roberto leaned back against the sofa's backrest and ran a hand through his hair.

He glanced from Naomi to Luca before he spoke again.

"Last night when I got home, Dino was there. He'd been waiting for me. I've never seen anyone in such a state. He looked as though he'd aged about ten years since the day before. He was a mess. So, I invited him in and gave him a stiff drink."

As though Signora Giana was summoned by the word "drink,"

she appeared in the doorway carrying a huge tray with their drinks and snacks.

Luca quickly got up to take the tray from her and brought it to the coffee table. Naomi removed a cluster of candles and the small bronze sculpture of an elephant Luca had given her. She put them underneath the coffee table out of the way, Luca placed the tray on the coffee table and poured a cup for Roberto.

As Roberto took his coffee from Luca, he resumed his account.

"Thanks, Luca. Well, it took a while, but what he told me wasn't only shocking, it explains a great deal of what's been going on.

"Turns out Fia had been leading him on for a good few years. I suspect she must've targeted him because he is your personal guard, Luca. And being a young guy and Fia being a beautiful girl, he fell head over heels in love with her. But he didn't have to spell out he soon realized how manipulative she is. He tried to break it off. But she threatened to blackmail him with a video she'd taken when they were in an intimate situation. He didn't want to lose his job and knew Armati discourages personal relationships at work."

Roberto took a sip of his coffee and nodded to Luca before speaking again.

"Seems your video isn't the first time she'd used that trick, Luca."

Luca put down his cup and sat back.

"Interesting. Though, the video Naomi received was a grand production, not merely a sex video. How did Fia pull that off? Did Dino know anything about it?"

Roberto nodded,

"Funny you should mention it. It was one reason Dino wanted to end it with Fia. He swore he had nothing to do with it. And I believed him. But do you remember Fia's little accomplice who'd barged into your office that morning with her phone taking pictures of the two of you?"

Luca nodded while Naomi looked questioningly at Roberto.

"Laura is one of the junior secretaries who worked with Fia. I don't know exactly what Fia has on her, but Dino told me Laura follows Fia around like a little puppy dog and does her every bidding. Laura is a whizz with technology, no doubt the reason for Fia's involvement with her. Dino said Laura was the creator of that video. She was at the party that night, and on Fia's instructions, videoed everything that happened with you and Fia."

Naomi clamped a hand over her mouth and shook her head. Despite her suspicions, she couldn't help feeling incredulous that anyone, even Fia, would stoop so low. But relief washed through her to discover she wasn't crazy for thinking Fia had been behind the video all along.

Luca put an arm around her shoulders and pulled her into his body as though he wanted to protect her from hearing the worst.

Roberto put down his coffee, leaned back against the sofa and sighed.

"I fear you were right, Naomi. The conversation you'd over-heard at Luigi's was between Fia and Laura. According to Dina, they were talking about how they'd drugged Luca that night with the express purpose of getting him into a compromising position."

Luca's jaw clenched.

"Vixens!"

Roberto stared intently at his friend.

"That they are, my friend.

"Dino said he'd arrived at Fia's place one night and overheard her and Laura, who was also there, talking about drugging you. That was the first he'd heard of it or of the video they'd made. I tell you, I've never seen a man as broken as Dino was last night. He must genuinely have loved Fia.

"Of course, I didn't know about his feelings or involvement with Fia when I appointed him to guard her after the police had let her go. She knew her way around him. Apparently, she'd told him she'd been unfairly dismissed. That's why she could get here yesterday morning to have a go at you, Naomi. Dino believed her and let her come here."

Naomi shook her head, a small smile of disbelief on her lips.

"Yes, Kerri mentioned she thought there was something going on between Fia and the guard. I guess she was right."

Roberto nodded.

"From the state of him, I guess Dino had realized Fia had been lying to him when he arrived here and saw for himself the chaos she'd caused."

Luca removed his arm from around his wife and poured more coffee for them.

"What I don't understand is why? Why the drugs? Why the video? Why the fire last night?"

Roberto accepted his coffee from Luca.

"I guess we'll never know for sure unless she confesses. But Dino believes she genuinely thought she could make you fall in love with her, Luca, that she could be Mrs Luca Armati. When you showed no interest in her, she took drastic measures and invited herself to your party that night. It was all pre-meditated, of course. She wasn't going to leave anything to chance apparently, according to what Dino overheard. If you wouldn't fall in love with her of your own volition, she was planning on blackmailing you into marrying her. But the girl must have a screw loose, because I can't imagine how anyone sane would think a plan like that might work. The classic bunny-boiler, don't you think?"

Luca noisily blew out his breath as he shook his head.

"I never imagined anything like this could ever happen to me. Where is she now?"

Roberto put down his cup before speaking.

"She's not in police custody, if that's what you were hoping."

Luca nodded, but Roberto continued before Luca could speak.

"They haven't been able to prove who started the fire yet. The fire marshal is still investigating it. But we know Fia was here posing as a waitress. That's not a crime in itself. So, to answer your question, Luca, she's at her house. But this time, I have two guards keeping an eye on her and I'm sure she has no relationship with either of them. They've been thoroughly briefed and informed she might try anything to get around them. Dino couldn't be more remorseful for the part he'd played in allowing Fia to cause such havoc. We must discuss what to do with him once my investigation is complete, Luca."

Naomi sat forward and placed a comforting hand on her husband's arm but directed her question at Roberto.

"What happens now?"

Roberto shrugged and leaned back into the sofa after taking a sip of coffee.

"I'll let you know, I guess. But you two should still leave. I believe it's the best thing to do. Dino's testimony is hearsay. It won't stand up in a court of law. There is still much to investigate."

CHAPTER 12

"*W*hat's the time?"

Noami and Kerri giggled and threw conspiratorial glances at each other.

Naomi didn't need to look at her watch again.

"It's about two minutes later than the last time you asked, Mr Armati."

Luca heaved his tall sun-bronzed body out of the pool and took long strides to where Naomi and Kerri were sitting just inside the Lapa. Both women reacted at the same time.

They jumped up and ran away squealing because Luca's intention to shake water all over them was clear in the mischievous glint in his eyes and his wicked smile. He ran after them and easily caught Naomi in a bear hug. Shaking his hair in her face and trying to get her as soaked as he was, he accomplished his goal easily. He was much stronger and struggle as she might she was well and truly caught in his arms. But she was laughing so much that she couldn't move, anyway. Luca kissed her all over her face and neck and ears and down her arms. His actions increased her laughing fit but in between gulping for air, she managed to plead with him.

"Stop...Luca...stop! I'll wet myself."

Luca threw back his head and laughed. His deep baritone resonated through Naomi where their bodies were still touching.

Over the sound of their laughter, the roar of a Cessna plane's engine was getting louder as it came closer to Desert Lodge.

As Luca was temporarily distracted by the sound of the plane, it meant Naomi could disentangle herself from her husband. She knew she looked exactly as drenched as he'd intended for her. But the Cessna was already landing behind the lodge, and there was no time to get back into a state of composure, first, before meeting it. Luca had slipped on his flip-flops and a t-shirt over his head, meanwhile, wet curls falling over his eyes.

He grabbed her hand.

"About time," he said as he ran and pulled her behind him.

Luca tried to hide his excitement at seeing his friend, but Naomi could feel his energy coursing through his body and into hers. She knew three months of Skyping and phone calls had been frustrating for Luca. No doubt, it was the same for Roberto. The men, whose bond was as close as that of blood brothers, were used to seeing each other every day since they were children. No one was surprised when Luca invited Roberto to Desert Lodge at the first opportunity.

Now, things had progressed well on the Fia front, Naomi knew Luca felt it was the least he could do to offer Roberto this short vacation.

Kerri followed them. Johan, who'd emerged from the guest lounge to see what jollity he was missing when the women shrieked at Luca's antics, quickly caught up with Kerri. He put an arm around his wife and followed his friends to welcome Roberto to Desert Lodge.

When the small sandstorm the Cessna had created died down, Luca took long strides to greet a smiling Roberto who emerged from the plane. His bag was in one hand and the other raised in greeting to the friends who'd come to meet him.

After Roberto had checked into his room and enjoyed a relaxing coffee with the others, Luca got up, evidently impatient to begin work before Roberto's travel weariness kicked in.

"Kerri, it's still okay to use your office, si?"

Kerri nodded and got up, too.

"Of course, Luca. I've arranged with Chef to have more coffee delivered there or whatever you need. How long do you think you'll be?"

She added quickly.

"Not that I'll need my office this afternoon. I was just-"

Luca understood what she meant but looked to Roberto, who shrugged before he spoke.

"We have quite a lot of Armati business to get through, nevermind the Fia issue. But I'll happily repeat news about Fia at dinner tonight.

Naomi couldn't help noticing Roberto wasn't smiling as he said the words. It didn't bode well, but she didn't want to think about it in case she was wrong.

After agreeing to meet back at the Lapa later, everyone went their separate ways.

Johan had to return to the elephant orphanage, and Naomi and Kerri paid the desert another visit, meanwhile.

The women took along tea and snacks and drove to the waterhole to distract themselves. They were bursting to know what news Roberto had brought of Fia. But they also knew he had important work issues to discuss with Luca. Their curiosity would just have to wait. Small talk didn't quell their impatience, so they ended up watching the surrounding wildlife in silence, each busy with her own thoughts. As they sat there with the desert sounds surrounding them and the sun on their faces, calm eventually and inevitably replaced their agitation.

Naomi marveled once again, as she'd done over the past few months, how much stronger her relationship with Luca now was. It had been strong before, but dealing with the challenges Fia had created, had resulted in an even more secure bond between her and Luca. The irony of Fia wanting the exact opposite, almost made Naomi feel sorry for her. Almost. But Naomi couldn't forgive the young woman for putting them through such an unnecessary stress. Instead, she felt grateful to Fia for facilitating the opportunity that cemented her bond with Luca so deeply and helped to make it utterly unbreakable. How Luca had raced home the day she'd received that video will forever stay with her. He did exactly the rights things and used the perfect words to make her feel safe, loved and adored by him. She appreciated it more than she had words to tell him.

Beside Naomi, Kerri yawned and stretched her arms above her head.

"You're quiet, hun. Don't tell me you're missing Modena?"

Naomi smiled.

"No. Funny, I haven't thought about Modena at all. I'm just enjoying being here. It still feels like I was only on vacation there."

"I can understand it. You'd need to be there longer to feel like it's your home, I guess. But I want to ask you something."

Naomi cast a questioning look at her friend.

"You don't usually ask to ask something. You usually just do it. What's up?"

"It's about Fia. And I don't want to remind you of what you'd left behind in Italy and what might be waiting for you on your return."

The question was clear in Naomi's eyes as she contemplated her friend.

Kerri frowned as though she was trying to plan the question in her mind, first, before putting it to Naomi.

"There's something I don't understand... Why were you so reluctant to press charges against Fia even when it became clear she was more than just a nuisance? I know there is no way I could've been as restrained as you've been."

Naomi moved around in her seat so she could face her friend.

A smile lit up her eyes.

"Yes, knowing you as I do, I'm sure Fia wouldn't have known what hit her. But don't think for a second it was easy for me."

She ran a hand through her hair as she got her thoughts together.

"I know this sounds stupid, but I underestimated her. Even though I had my suspicions, and we know now your instinct about her having a thing with Dino was right, the whole thing felt surreal, like a dream. In my mind, I genuinely didn't think it would escalate in the way it did. Instead, I assumed she would just go away when she saw her actions had no impact on Luca and me."

Kerri put a hand on her friend's arm.

"But I don't think she's quite stable, do you?"

"I know why you're saying it but... When it comes to love, are any of us sane? Although, you may have a point because she seems more obsessed with Luca rather than in love with him. But to answer your question. I didn't want to press charges because I genuinely thought she'd go away of her own accord. And you know me. I firmly believe if you let something go, it reduces its hold on you. Conversely, if you pursue it, you become consumed by it. I didn't want that for Luca or myself."

She gave a little laugh.

"Or perhaps it's just me?"

Kerri glanced at her friend.

"When did you become so wise? You're right. That's exactly what happens. One only has to look at Fia to see the truth of that idea."

"True. She's the perfect example of what I don't want to be. But I can't take all the credit for my belief. It's a concept deeply ingrained in the culture of the San people. Having spent much of my youth with them, I guess it's rubbed off on me."

Kerri nodded, her mind already racing ahead.

"I wonder what will happen to Fia? I really hope Roberto has sorted out something that feels like justice. Do you know what I mean?"

Naomi turned to face the steering wheel again and started the engine.

"I know exactly what you mean. It's what I hope, too. But talking of Roberto, I guess we'd better get back. They might have finished their meeting by now."

Naomi and Kerri arrived back at the lodge at the same time as Johan drove up beside them. But there was still no sign of Luca and Roberto when the trio went looking for them in the Lapa.

Long shadows had started to cast their welcome coolness over the lodge.

Guests were getting ready to go on sunset safaris, and Kerri went off to do her managerial duties, checking everyone had what they wanted and were happy.

Johan, sweaty and dusty from working with the orphaned ellies, went to his and Kerri's room for a shower and a change of clean clothes.

It still felt odd to Naomi that Auntie Elsa's old room had been turned into an oasis for Johan and Kerri. Naomi's room had been redecorated into the perfect home from home for her and Luca. She made her way there to get changed into her bathing suit. The pool had looked far too inviting. Now, that most of the guests would be away from the lodge, she'd have it all to herself.

~

The stars were already blinking against a rapidly darkening sky, and the crickets' song was getting louder, when Roberto and Luca emerged from the office. Their jovial mood of earlier had evaporated. Instead, they wore frowns between their tired eyes and the weight of their discussion. Their demeanor didn't fill Naomi's heart with optimism.

Johan's voice boomed over the pool.

"There you are. We were just thinking you've gone back to Italy and forgot to tell us."

Johan roared at his own joke, and somehow, it broke through the heaviness Luca and Roberto had brought with them into the Lapa.

As though noticing where he was for the first time, Roberto blinked and looked around.

"What's that intoxicating smell?"

The others laughed at his expression before Johan rescued him.

"That's the dinner you nearly missed, Roberto, man. Come, sit. Sit. I'll get you a beer meantime."

Luca and Roberto took their places at the table while Johan went to the bar to get beers for everyone. A waitress appeared pulling a trolley piled high with steaming plates of delicious barbecue meats and salads.

Naomi was grateful for Kerri's foresight in arranging for only their small party to use the Lapa that night.

Throughout dinner, Johan regaled them with stories of the ellies.

Roberto was evidently enjoying his meal. His eyes twinkled as he watched Johan talking and laughing at his own jokes.

After another particularly descriptive tale of the ellies's antics, Roberto smiled before he spoke.

"You have a wonderful energy, Johan. The orphans are lucky to have you watch over them."

Johan accepted the compliment with grace and launched into a story about the tactics he'd used to keep Luca awake on the flight from Italy.

After Roberto had finished his meal, pushed back his plate

and sat back in his chair, he regarded his friends around the table.

"I know you're all dying to know what's happened with Fia."

Everyone stopped eating at once and sat forward ready to listen.

"You already know many things. Fia's accomplice, Laura, had helped her to buy the viagra and amphetamines from the internet with which to drug Luca at his party. Together with alcohol, it could have been a recipe for disaster."

Naomi's heart beat very fast at the thought Luca could have died from the concoction of drugs and drink. He sensed her anxiety and took her hand in his under the table giving it a comforting squeeze.

Roberto looked at his friend.

"A good thing Luca isn't a big drinker."

Luca's head was down, the frown between his eyes the only sign of his turbulent emotions.

Roberto sighed before he continued.

"All of you know Laura was in charge of the video. Somehow, Fia discovered Laura is a lesbian and used that information to her advantage. During interrogation, it became clear Laura was in love with Fia which explains why she did whatever Fia wanted. It includes taking pictures on her phone the morning Fia went to Luca's office. It also includes helping Fia to masquerade as a waitress at the villa the night of your celebration, Johan and Kerri. Evidently, Laura is the niece of the wedding planner you'd hired. That is why no alarm bells rang with anyone before the fire. It was again Laura who'd helped Fia to build what turned out essentially to be bombs to start the fire."

Kerri interrupted.

"That's why everyone appeared so traumatized. I couldn't figure it out at the time."

Roberto nodded at her.

"Yes, although small enough to be smuggled into the marquee

in their uniforms, the devices were bombs, nonetheless. Of course, it was a terrible shock for the staff working there at the time. It caused as much panic and chaos as possible so the two girls could escape without being noticed while destroying the marquee and the evening's event completely. They had to get away of their own accord as, by this time, Fia could no longer count on Dino, and she knew it."

It was Johan's turn to interrupt.

"It was upsetting. But actually, Fia did us a favor because the evening turned out even better than we could have imagined. And my wife and Naomi even got a lucrative business deal out of it when Enzo agreed to rent them a section of the castle for their Namibian/Italian wedding planning business. It was such a throwaway conversation with Enzo. I'm not sure it would've happened had the celebration in the marquee gone ahead."

Kerri and Naomi smiled at Johan.

Kerri placed a hand on Johan's arm.

"You're right, darling. I don't think it would've happened either."

She turned to look at Roberto.

"Thank you for the information, Roberto. It's fascinating to hear how it all happened. But I can't wait to find out what actually happened to Fia."

Roberto's smile was indulgent.

"I realize it's difficult to wait while I wade through the background stuff, first, Kerri. But it's important for you to know so Fia's sentence will make sense."

Kerri let out an exaggerated sigh and leaned back in her chair.

"Well, thank goodness there is a sentence, and she's not getting off scot-free."

At her words, a titter went through the small party at the table. It temporarily broke the seriousness on their faces.

Roberto nodded at Kerri.

"Oh, yes. There is a sentence. But before I get to it, I want to add the judge at first considered sentencing Fia to six months in prison. As you might imagine, the case has generated a lot of media exposure."

He glanced at Luca and Naomi.

"That's why I'm so pleased you two could escape it. By the time you return to Modena, people's attention would've moved on elsewhere, and you can get on with your lives in peace."

Naomi cleared her throat before speaking.

"But six months doesn't sound that long. Why only six months?"

Roberto nodded again to show he agreed with Naomi and he intended to explain.

"Yes, six months doesn't sound long. But Fia hasn't helped herself. She pleaded insanity. The judge found while she was under an insane delusion, she knew she was acting contrary to the law. Six months is currently the longest sentence she could have received in such a case. But as she'd pleaded insanity, it had to be investigated further. It turns out that Fia has a long history of mental illness and this isn't the first time she'd drugged and videoed an unsuspecting potential husband. Shortly after leaving school, she did the same thing to one of her teachers with whom she'd had an affair."

Everyone around the table, including Luca, watched Roberto with astonishment clear on their faces.

Roberto turned to Luca.

"I told you earlier I had some surprising information for you, didn't I?"

Luca snorted.

"Mph, so you did, but I never expected this."

Kerri couldn't contain herself any longer. She sat forward, her body alive with eagerness.

"Please, Roberto. Put us out of our misery. What happened?"

Roberto smiled briefly before continuing.

"Sorry, Kerri. I didn't mean to drag it out deliberately. I

thought you all needed to know the facts, first. Fia has been found not guilty by reason of insanity."

Naomi's sharp intake of breath mirrored everyone else's shock and fears.

But Roberto held up a hand.

"It's why I said Fia didn't help herself. As a result of having been found not guilty because of insanity, she'll be confined to a mental institution indefinitely. If she'd just pleaded guilty, she might have been free after only six months."

Roberto leaned back in his chair and placed both hands behind his head.

"I think, ladies and gentleman, justice has been served."

There was a moment's silence before everyone spoke altogether.

But Johan's voice boomed above the others'.

"This calls for a celebration. You're fantastic, Roberto, man. Thank you for everything."

Johan got up and shook Roberto's hand before he went to the bar to fetch some champagne.

Luca got up and pulled Roberto from his chair, hugging him and kissing him on both cheeks over and over again.

Kerri came to hug Naomi whose green eyes glittered with tears of gratitude.

Long after the others had gone to bed, Luca and Naomi sat side-by-side in the Lapa. They watched the thousands of stars the Milky Way had generously strewn across the black sky.

Luca's arms felt comforting and warm around Naomi's shoulders, and she leaned her head on his shoulder.

Luca's voice was soft when he spoke.

"Satisfied, Mrs Armati?"

"Satisfied, Mr Armati. You?"

She could feel his nod in the dark.

Far in the night was the sound of an elephant trumpeting, perhaps his song to his beloved.

As though Luca had the same thought, he pulled Naomi closer to sit on his lap. She returned his soft, loving kisses, breathing him in. Both relished this moment, this sublime knowing they'd found the other half of their soul in each other and nothing and no one could ever break them apart.

HEAT IN THE DESERT

The second Saira stepped off the plane, the heat struck her forcibly, a stark reminder of the other, emotionally sweltering situation she'd left behind in London although she couldn't blame that on the climate there.

To say the cold London weather hadn't prepared her for the instant struggle to breathe in the Namibian heat was the understatement of the year. Even spending vacations in the humid heat of their Indian family farm was nothing compared to this.

How was she going to live and work here for the next few months? She'd just have to get the job over and done with as quickly as possible, that's how.

Saira followed her fellow passengers along the tarmac to the airport's entrance. She couldn't help noticing the heat waves forming in the air ahead of her when normally she would have expected to see those in the far distance. To add to the discomfort of her long flight, a trickle of sweat ran down her back, causing her white silk shirt to stick to her body.

What had possessed her to wear silk?

She hoped sweat marks weren't visible beneath her armpits. While her well-cut black trousers had felt comfortable and smart in London, here it clung to her sweaty legs and made her feel as though she was suffocating from the bottom up.

But her case was heavy, the wheels kept catching in the cracks on the tarmac, and after the long flight, she was too exhausted to care about her appearance.

The blast from the air condition as she walked through the airport's doors was almost too cold. Goosebumps formed all over her body. Still, she welcomed the respite. The heat had pressed down on her, making even her smallest movements a battle against lethargy.

Not for the first time, she wondered if it was all worth it? Would such an effort even register with Max Galbraith? He'd made it clear he wanted something special to sell to a large terrestrial television channel, and he didn't care which one. Of course, with his reputation, he'd most likely have the pick of the bunch.

Saira couldn't prevent the anxiety rising into her chest.

Thoughts of her boss linked to thoughts of Jonathan. Would she have severed the relationship by now if Jonathan wasn't Max's son?

She tossed her hair back as though to toss all thoughts of Jonathan from her mind.

Why had she been so reluctant to take this assignment? Wasn't this just the opportunity she'd needed to prove herself to Max once and for all? Oh, who was she kidding? Hadn't she been thinking this might be what she'd needed to prove to herself she could do it, do her own thing?

But the voices of the naysayers assaulted her mind at once, the loudest was her own.

"You're too young to start your own company?"

"You owe Max a few more years after all he's done for you."

"Be sensible and follow a proper career, one that can give you security for your future."

"What if you fail?"

Her parents' trusting, sincere faces flitted past her mind's eye. Hadn't they always taught her through their example? But their plans for her had never included working in the television industry. The path they'd wanted for her corresponded with theirs, a lawyer or something in investment banking. Their worried eyes carried the questions they'd never asked.

Saira sighed away the images in her head and followed her fellow passengers down the long corridor.

At least the rigmarole of going through passport control brought extended relief from the heat in the form of air conditioning.

Saira expected someone with a plaque bearing her name to be waiting for her in arrivals. Instead, she heard her name being called over the airport's PA system.

She swore under her breath. The long flight and the sudden heat outside had taken its toll. She was hungry and thirsty and didn't feel like having to deal with a problem now. But the sooner she got it over and done with, the better.

She shifted her bag to her right shoulder to give the left one time to recover from where the straps had cut into her. Pulling her suitcase behind her on the left side, kept her handbag in place on her shoulder. She felt a twinge of gratitude for small mercies.

Apart from the information agent, only one other person stood next to the counter as she approached it. Saira assumed he had to be there for her as he looked like he might be local, his sun darkened skin and safari uniform giving that impression.

She prayed Desert Lodge wasn't too far away. Every pore in her body screamed for a shower and a soft bed afterwards. She'd think about work tomorrow.

As she extended her hand towards him, she took a step back in surprise when his green eyes locked onto hers. She hadn't expected him to be so striking and when his eyes ran over her body before capturing her eyes again, she felt a small flutter in her stomach.

Her mouth was suddenly dry, but she remained polite and professional even though her voice sounded tight to her ears.

"Hi, I'm Saira from MaxPix."

Her conscious effort to lower her voice at the end of the phrase gave a sense of confidence, a trick she'd learned to use when she was tired, so she'd be taken seriously.

When the man's hand enveloped hers, she hadn't expected the immediate connection she felt as his hand touched hers.

His voice sounded relaxed and musical to her ears, and far friendlier than he appeared because his greeting contained no smile or warmth.

"Gerard. Desert Lodge. Follow me."

Then, Gerard turned and walked toward the exit.

Saira settled her handbag more comfortably on her shoulder and pulling her suitcase behind her, followed his tall, muscular figure.

She was too surprised and too tired to comment. The man was a rude baffoon, clearly. He hadn't even offered to help her with her luggage.

Bristling at his behavior, Saira had to admit he was an interesting-looking man, but she didn't appreciate his brusqueness.

Briefly, she wondered if this behavior was the norm in Namibia but dismissed the thought as soon as it had popped into her head. She'd been in contact with Naomi and Kerri at Desert Lodge over the past few months, and although very different from each other, both seemed friendly and easy to work with.

Saira had to walk faster than she'd wanted to keep up with Gerard. But the exercise woke her up a little, and she felt a spurt of energy flood through her body.

Hopefully, her work at Desert Lodge wouldn't involve Gerard. God knows, she had quite enough on her plate right now and could do without the usual stress of dealing with difficult clients. Not that Desert Lodge was a client. Not yet. But she hoped to persuade them to allow her carte blanche when shooting a compelling tv series there. All she had to do was get their signatures on an agreement and then shoot a spectacular pilot to sell. She had to admit the place sounded interesting. Although, when Max Galbraith had talked her into this trip, she could think of a thousand better things to do with her time than traipsing around in the desert. Now, after her first resistance to the project, she looked forward to it.

The long flight here had given her ample time to consider once more the repercussions of her decision to accept Max's offer. But she wasn't stupid. She knew Max had given her the assignment because she was the only young female producer at MaxPix and this pilot was about weddings. She could have been offended. She should have been offended. But wasn't it just normal for the industry, this sort of sexism? It made her want to scream at them all to sod right off. Instead, it renewed her resolve to go after her dream. It meant ignoring everyone else's advice. But it wasn't their dream, was it?

But this was also the chance to get away from Jonathan. The flight had given her time to think about Jonathan and her future with or without him.

She was still tormented with the thoughts in her head when she realized they'd reached the exit. She steeled herself for the intense heat that waited outside the building. But as Gerard opened the door, it felt as though the sun tried show off exactly how brutal it could be.

Once again, Saira fought for every breath as they made their way from the air-conditioned building to the small Cessna plane sitting to the left of the airport.

Gerard opened the door for her and surprised her by taking her bags and stowing them behind her seat before helping her up into her seat and closing the door. He walked around the plane to the other side as though he didn't even feel the heat, but it followed him and blasted into the small cabin when he opened the door and slid into the seat beside her.

Was this how it would be the whole time she'd be here? How would she endure it? If there was a hell, it must be this.

Gerard fiddled with knobs and the sudden roar and shaking of the plane made Saira sink into her seat and grip the armrests.

Together, in the close quarters of the cockpit, Saira became acutely aware of Gerard's imposing physique. When his leg touched hers, concern fluttered through her mind. How would she manage the journey with him sitting so close? She moved her leg away and tried to think of something else to distract herself.

She was just about to ask Gerard how long the flight to Desert Lodge was, but he'd already donned his headset and was talking to the control tower about taking off.

The knot in Saira's stomach became tighter as they started to taxi down the airstrip. She could feel her hands getting sweaty but couldn't let go of the grip she had on the armrests. The plane felt too small, too exposed, too much like a tin can.

When Gerard opened the throttle, and the plane started to race down the airstrip, Saira shut her eyes as tight as she could and felt her lips mimicking the action. The plane wobbled as they took to the air and the engines screamed their protest at having to lift away from the ground, echoing Saira's feelings.

Saira didn't believe in prayer but prayed anyway even though she wasn't aware of actual words. She couldn't believe she'd thought getting into such a flimsy-looking thing was a good idea. She didn't want this to be her last day on earth. But as the wobbling died down, and she felt the plane leveling out, becoming steadier,, she opened her eyes.

Out of the corner of her eye, she could've sworn she saw an amused smile flit across Gerard's face but she must have imagined it, or he was a master at hiding his emotions because he seemed serious when he nodded at her and handed her a headset.

Once she'd put it on, she could hear Gerard's voice in her ears.

"Are you okay? Do you need anything? There's water behind your seat."

Wow, the silent one could speak.

Saira nodded and found a bottle of water in a small refrigerated cabinet behind her seat. She unscrewed the top and took a long welcoming slug of the cool liquid. She held the bottle against her forehead and tipped it over against her wrists so that the water would reach her pulse without pouring out everywhere. Then, she poured a tiny amount into her hand and ran it over her neck, decolletage, cheeks and forehead. It seemed to work. She felt revived immediately, and no longer parched. The fact that a breeze was blowing through the windows Gerard had opened a little helped.

She could feel Gerard's eyes on her but when she looked at him, he was staring ahead into the distance.

Feeling better, gave her the courage to peek through the window at her side.

They were on the outskirts of Windhoek. As she watched, the houses and green of the trees and lawns and blue swimming pools made way for the unending stretch of desert sand to the horizon.

Saira had seen many pictures and documentaries about Namibia and knew it was beautiful. But the scene that met her eyes was breath-taking. Red sand dunes sprinkled with dried yellow grasses and the odd tree, stretched into the distance to meet a cloudless blue sky. The only other moving thing, as far as she could see, was the shadow of the plane that followed them as it undulated over the sand dunes below.

Again, she wondered how long it was before they'd reach Desert Lodge, but before she could ask, Gerard surprised her.

"We'll arrive at Desert Lodge in about an hour. Relax and enjoy the view. We'll be flying over some interesting terrain."

His unusual green eyes rested on her for a moment before he looked ahead again, his face a mask once more.

Saira stared at the handsome man beside her.

For someone never without words, her mind had drawn an unexpected blank. All her questions had evaporated in his gaze.

The expression in his eyes had reached out and touched her heart in a way she'd never experienced before.

She shook her head.

For goodness' sake, she wasn't even at Desert Lodge yet and already potential trouble followed her. She didn't need any kind of complication, and certainly not this kind. Hadn't she just left trouble like this behind with Jonathan in London?

Suddenly, a loud pop brought Saira back to the present. The plane started to shake at once. A thin, pale plume of smoke blew past them.

When she turned to look at Gerard, she saw that his knuckles were white on the yoke and his eyes narrowed in concentration.

His voice sounded deliberately calm when he spoke.

"We need to do an emergency landing. Make sure you fasten your seatbelt."

A WORD FROM ANGELINA

Thank you for reading *Love In Modena*.

If you enjoyed it, you might also like the other books in the series.

In the first novel, *Under A Namibian Sky*, we meet Luca and Naomi for the first time. It is the story of how this unlikely couple met and fell in love.

In the next novel, *Heat In The Desert*, we again meet Luca and Naomi, but also more characters as the story of Desert Lodge unfolds. And there are more books in to come in the series.

Building a relationship with my readers is the very best thing about writing. Occasionally, I send out newsletters with details on new releases, special offers and other bits of news relating to my novels.

If you sign up to my newsletter, I will send you this **FREE** content:

1.A free thought-sheet from Naomi, the orphaned elephant, an introduction to the novella, *Diary of Naomi, Desert Elephant*.

2.The first five audio chapters of *Under A Namibian Sky* read by me.

As all authors, I appreciate enormously your short review on Amazon or Goodreads stating why you liked the novel. I cannot stress how important reviews are. They enable novels like Under A Namibian Sky to live in the world.

I LOVE to hear from readers, so please feel free to contact me via Amazon, Facebook, twitter or my website.

www.angelinakalahari.com

https://www.amazon.com/Angelina-Kalahari/e/ B014HLBJ2K/ref=ntt_dp_epwbk_0

https://www.facebook.com/authorangelinakalahari/

https://twitter.com/angelinakalhari

You can also contact me directly at:
angelina@angelinakalahari.com
I read every email.

THE INSPIRATION BEHIND

LOVE IN MODENA

Love In Modena is the follow-up novella from *Under A Namibian Sky*.

I have to admit I was genuinely thrilled when so many readers said they'd enjoyed reading *Under A Namibian Sky*.

Not long after the novel was published, I started receiving emails asking what happens to Luca and Naomi once they move to Italy.

Readers' curiosity sparked my own, and I couldn't help wondering how Naomi was settling in, or how being married would affect Luca's lifestyle. As they'd got married rather quickly, perhaps it was a shock to those who'd known Luca to be free and single.

Love In Modena was born.

I had a notion about what their life together might be like, that their love would grow stronger and they'd navigate life's ups and downs buoyed by the strength of their love.

Naomi remarked the passion of love could make any of us crazy. But even I couldn't have predicted someone like Fia. She caught me by surprise as much as I hope she did you.

I'm very grateful I've never had to deal with someone quite

like her in my own life. Though, unfortunately, I've had a few similar experiences when I was still singing professionally. It was beyond scary.

Usually, elsewhere in their lives, such people seem just like you or me. That's the scary part, don't you think?

Let me know if you've ever experienced something like it. I'd be very interested to know.

ALSO BY ANGELINA

FIRST IN THE DESERT LOVE SERIES

UNDER A NAMBIAN SKY

"The story was so compelling, I simply couldn't put this book down." - Amazon reviewer.

Naomi Smith is an ordinary young woman - until Luca Armati appears and shatters her world.

They couldn't be more different. She is a safari guide at Desert Lodge where life revolves around her beloved desert. He is the heir apparent to the Italian supercar dynasty that bears his family name, used to the glitz and glam that goes with his destiny.

Only one thing connects them - each holds a secret they'd rather not share. But when their secrets are exposed, the barrier that kept them apart shatters.

If you enjoy novels by M. M. Kay or Mary Stewart, then you will love Angelina Kalahari's Under A Namibian Sky, an emotionally riveting contemporary romance.

Explore Under A Namibian Sky, the first novel in the captivating Desert Love series today.

NEXT IN THE DESERT LOVE SERIES

DAIRY OF NAOMI, DESERT ELEPHANT

Elephants in Namibia are the toughest in Africa. But orphaned elephants are the toughest still. And they need to be.

All elephants must travel great distances to find food to live on and they're renowned for their magnificent memories.

In this novella, discover what happens when they find the people responsible for making them orphans?

HEAT IN THE DESERT

Saira Kahn is an ambitious television producer who has visions of creating her own production company where she will be in charge of her path in life.

When Saira is tasked to shoot a pilot for wedding ceremonies at Desert Lodge in Namibia, not only does she see the opportunity to have her desire come true, but she also meets her prince, desert guide, Gerard Fredriks. She has to battle with herself, her ex and Gerard's secret for her freedom to pursue both passions.

Now, with the help of Gerard, Saira must find a way to destroy her old self and her old life, so she can be free to live the life of her dreams with a man she couldn't have dreamed.

THE HEALING TOUCH

"A book full of surprises...this book was, for me, an exploration of how profound human love can be, how joy can exist despite the pain of loss." - Amazon reviewer.

Isabelle Cooper is a talented, complex fifty-five old performer going through her menopause.

Caught in an emotionally cold and sexless marriage, Isabelle yearns for more.

On the advice of her confidante, James, with whom she has an extremely close but platonic relationship,

Isabelle embarks on an affair with Angelo Antoniou.

Isabella's heart is ripped in two when James suddenly dies. Bereft of this intense relationship, Isabelle must learn to live in a world without James, trapped between an unhappy marriage, and her loving relationship with Angelo.

Inspired by true events, *The Healing Touch* is a mesmerising story of loss, heartbreak, passion, and love in many guises, a gripping read you won't want to put down. Funny, devastating, and uplifting by turns, *The Healing Touch* will leave you yearning to experience the perfect love yourself.

A HUGE THANK YOU

To best editorial team in the world – Christine, Elizabeth, John, Susie, Julia, Irma, Linda, Judy and Kumi – thank you so much for reading, commenting, suggesting and helping me to create a world in which to escape and to bask for a while.

Without you, this novella would not have become the story it has. I'm grateful you asked all the right questions and helped me to become a better writer.

To Jane Dixon- Smith for the most romantic cover.

ABOUT ANGELINA

Author photograph ©www.Bobieh.com

Angelina Kalahari has worked for over thirty-five years as an operatic soprano and stage director around the world.

She received recognition for her contribution to the music, culture and economy of the UK from Queen Elizabeth II at Buckingham Palace.

Angelina has always regarded herself as a storyteller, either through music or through acting and directing. She honed her storytelling skills from a young age, writing and telling stories to her siblings at bed time. It became a habit through the years. She has many finished novels, children's stories and plays. Her publishing journey as an indie author began with The Healing Touch, a story based on true events.

Born in Namibia, and having lived all over the world, she currently lives in London, UK, with her husband, her fur cat daughter, a rapidly diminishing population of house spiders and a smallish herd of dust bunnies.

Printed in Great Britain
by Amazon

45124094R00078